Jimgrim and, the Lost Trooper

Classics by Talbot Mundy

Jimgrim and the Affair in Araby
Jimgrim & the Seventeen Thieves of El-Kalil
Jimgrim and Allah's Peace
Jimgrim and the Woman Ayisha
Jimgrim and a Secret Society
Jimgrim, Moses, and Mrs Aintree
Jimgrim and the Lost Trooper
The Gray Mahatma
The Ivory Trail
Caesar Dies
Queen Cleopatra
Guns of the Gods
The Nine Unknown
Rung Ho!

by Johnston McCulley

Black Star
The Mark of Zorro
The Spider Strain and Other Tales from the Pulps
Tales of Thubway Tham

by Robert E. Howard

The Complete Action Stories
Gates of Empire
Graveyard Rats
Moon of Skulls
Shadow Kingdoms
Treasures of Tartary
Waterfront Fists

*For more information and
a list of all the Wildside Press titles,
please see our web site:*
www.wildsidebooks.com

Jimgrim and, the Lost Trooper

Talbot Mundy

WILDSIDE PRESS

JIMGRIM AND THE LOST TROOPER

First published in *Adventure,* May 30th, 1922
Published by Wildside Press LLC.
www.wildsidepress.com

Chapter I

"Talk about transmuting elements —"

H ow can you begin a tale at the beginning, when it has as many beginnings as there are people in it? I don't see that these critics who make literary laws have done much else than shut out two-thirds of the best tales by making it impossible to tell them.

At any rate, as I'm telling this one; and as nobody need listen if he doesn't like, I'm going to begin it where I please, which happens to be in Berlin, Germany, which I visited long enough after the Boer War for men who fought all through it, to show themselves there without having to have police protection.

My business is prospecting, and I hadn't made my little pile in those days — hadn't attained, in other words, to that only essential of contentment in this world: the ability as well as the inclination and the right to suit yourself as to what you'll do next, where you'll go, and how.

My particular pet delight is independence. But in those days I was trying to get a syndicate of Prussian *vons* and *zus* to finance an undertaking in what was then known as German East Africa. Looking back through the smoke of adventurous years I should say now that it would have been about as easy to persuade the U.S. Government to finance a claimant to the throne of France. I cooled my heels, spent money in a very bad hotel, and dare say I should have been insulted finally, if it weren't for my odd inch or so above six feet and the muscle that carries it upright. Even in those days the Prussians weren't openly rude to any one they weren't sure they could lick.

But I made a profit, for I met an Australian named Jeremy

Ross. It was worth a trip half around the world to make that man's acquaintance.

He was swearing at the methods of the same hotel proprietor and trying to tap the same financial sluices. We had two common grievances, which is sufficient basis for friendship in most circumstances; and, as we both were, comparatively speaking, broke, we walked about together a good deal, seeing what Berliners thought were sights, while the syndicate of *vons* and *zus* considered how to put one over on us — an entirely vain devotion of super-thought on their part, as well as a waste of our time.

Even in those days I had reached the point of tolerating other people's manners and notions right up to the chalk-line where they trespass on my liberty. But Jeremy Ross hadn't traveled as much, or met as many weird varieties as I had of the "manners" that "mayketh man."

Having served through the Boer War as a trooper in the First Australian Horse, he had a profound contempt for, and enmity against all officers who were not Australians risen from the ranks. But he didn't include all Australian officers in his catalog of the blessed by any means, having, as he put it, "eaten dirt from twenty-five too many of them."

"Talk about transmuting elements," said Jeremy. "Turning iron into gold is nothing to it. Take a chap who's a good mining-mate and a decent trooper, with no more use for the airs of officers than you've got, put a couple of imitation bronze stars on his shoulder, and you've turned him into a cocky ass, who'll slate you for fatigue if you tell him as much as where he came from and where he'd go if he'd take advice. Officers ought to be elected, that's what I think; and I can think as good as any one."

The sight of a three-inch red collar with gold lace on it to Jeremy was more irritating than a red flag to a black hull. A monocle acted on him as fulminate of mercury does on dynamite. So a jaunt shoulder-to-shoulder with him through the streets of Berlin was hardly a soporific. He took to imitating the swagger of the Prussian officers, with a silver coin stuck in his eye by way of emphasis. And Jeremy Ross is noticeable — a regular "corn-stalk," still wearing his big felt hat — lean, long-legged, striding like a horseman, none too comfortable on his feet; a handsome fellow, whom the women glanced at twice, which in itself was good ground for a quarrel in the Prussia of those days. So the Prussians had to notice him.

Still, somehow or other I contrived to keep him out of actual difficulties, even when he refused to give up his chair at a restaurant table in order that a party of Uhlan officers might have the corner of the beer-garden to themselves. I daresay the size of the two of us, added to our obvious unity of determination, had something to do with the officers' haughty retirement from the scene; but the proprietor wouldn't serve us after that, and Jeremy's wrath boiled over. He reached the conclusion that all Prussian arrogance was bluff, and when we strode out together after half-an-hour I knew that trouble was inevitable. But I liked him finely, and stood by.

It came even quicker than I expected. We were walking up a street that leads into Unter den Linden, remarking the free figure and neat ankles of an American girl going the same way about twenty yards in front of us. The sight started Jeremy to bragging about the female loveliness of New South Wales.

"None like 'em! None like 'em anywhere. A man couldn't be a polygamist in New South. One of our girls is worth a hundred from anywhere else in the world, and do your own picking. I'm going home again. A man's a fool to leave Australia."

The girl ahead of us was a tourist obviously. She was carrying parcels in both arms and had a camera slung over her shoulder by a strap. She was unused to Berlin, for she tried to take the wall of a monocled, high collared *von* in cavalry uniform who came clinking his saber and spurs down-street. I suppose nobody but the traffic cop in her home city had ever challenged her right of way before.

Well, the Prussian behaved according to type. He bore what he had been taught to think was dignity in mind, shouldered her out into the middle of the side-walk, knocking both parcels from her hands; and then he smirked at her with a view to starting flirtation. According to the code, she ought to have felt flattered by his attention; but being merely an American, uneducated in such matters, and seeing he made no attempt to spoil his corset by stooping to pick up the parcels, she looked about for a man. She seemed bewildered — hardly indignant at first — I think she was too much taken by surprise for that. The Prussian probably mistook her blush for a symptom of admiration for himself, for he murmured something and tried to take her arm.

She shook herself free of him at almost exactly the same second that Jeremy's fist took the Prussian in the jaw, sending him crupper over neck into the gutter. And it proved entirely characteristic of Jeremy that he ignored the Prussian forthwith, picked up the lady's parcels, and began a flirtation in his own way, on his own account. You'd have thought, if there had been time to think, that no such incident as spoiling a Prussian's dignity had ever taken place in his young life.

The Prussian didn't do much thinking. He was automatic. He scrambled to his feet, livid and bristling with all the rage he felt entitled to, and drew his saber. He didn't shout, or even swear. He had seen Jeremy and me together, and it was all one to him which of us had struck him. He came for the nearest of us, which happened to be me. And I didn't do much thinking either.

A man with a long saber is at a disadvantage at close quarters against any one with strength enough to use his hands as nature intended. I don't like bloodshed, particularly mine, so I took his toy away from him and broke it. I have been told since that that is considered a horrible indignity to put on a military person, and if I had realized as much at the time I dare say I wouldn't have broken the thing. I could have thrown it across the street, for instance. However, the harm was done.

Most of the mere civilians in sight proved their meanness by scattering for cover — didn't want to be called as witnesses, most likely. The only non-military gent who took an interest in the proceedings was a cabman, who drove past, turned and drove back again, willing to be anybody's friend at so much per. I gave the Prussian the two pieces of his sword, supposing he would enjoy making himself scarce at once, and signaled to the cabman to come and get him. But there were lots of things I didn't know in those days.

Jeremy was still talking to the girl — Miss Eliot I remember her name was. Honestly, I believe he had almost forgotten the whole incident. When the Prussian beckoned and a policeman came running with drawn sword, Jeremy didn't realize in the least that he was the goal — or rather, that the nearest jail was goal, and we three meant for footballs.

Several officers passed across the street half a block away, and our friend with the broken sword shouted to them. I knew enough German to get the gist of his remarks, and enough of politics to be aware that jail is no place from which to address your embassy, if you hope for satisfactory results. Besides, five more officers were straining their corset laces badly in a hurry to help their man; even with Jeremy to aid me, I couldn't take all their swords away. It was time now to act first and think afterwards.

The policeman was loud-mouthed and importunate. He

ordered us, Miss Eliot included, to march to the jail in front of him, and seemed to expect us to do it. I'm told we broke no less than nine laws by refusing to obey him; he brandished his sword in my face, but did not strike, and I believe the ass thought I was trying to help him when I seized Jeremy by the neck and shook him, to make him see sense. He wanted to stay there and fight all Berlin.

I caught the eye of the cabman, who drew up as close to us as he dared on the far side of the street. It did not take any persuading to get Miss Eliot into the cab, but I had to use violence on Jeremy, who has never since quite forgiven me for spoiling what he swears would have been a gorgeous victory. He went into the cab backwards, using bad words freely.

That sort of thing was evidently not unknown in Berlin, for the cabman needed no instructions. He whipped the pretty good horse to a gallop, and turned two corners before speaking. Then, slowing down to a trot as he turned a third corner, he leaned back to drive his bargain. He said he supposed that the *gnadige Herrschaften* had the British Embassy in mind.

But Jeremy and I were as one man in denouncing that suggestion. "The whole British Empire isn't worth a damn to a chap in trouble," laughed Jeremy. "They'd simply hand us over to the Square-heads. Maybe yes, if we had coronets embroidered on our underwear, but the socks I stole from a duke in the Boer War made the squadron jealous on the trooper going home, so I auctioned 'em off to the crew and as like as not they're in Hongkong or Yokohama. No, we can't pose as dukes. Let's try your embassy."

He chuckled while he talked, as if we had all played hookey from school and were having a gorgeous time. The cabman demanded a thousand marks, which I suppose was about the tariff in the circumstances; but Jeremy knew German pretty well, and offered to gamble with him — two hundred marks or nothing. He hadn't a trace of fear of consequences, and proved it by getting out to walk when the cabman turned obstinate; whereat a settlement was soon reached; we agreed on a hundred and fifty marks as the fare, and reached the United States Embassy streets ahead of the news.

The ambassador was out of town, as luck would have it; he might have been diffident, especially as one of us was an Australian. But there was a secretary there, whose aunt or somebody came from Miss Eliot's home-town, and what with the girl's influence, and Jeremy's chuckles, we had him convinced before the military telephoned. They had drawn the British Embassy blank by that time as well as all the leading hotels, and were growing furious.

I don't know the full extent of the lies that that good secretary told, and I certainly won't tell his name, for he did his duty and deserves a curtain. But I heard him say over the phone that we were all three intimate friends of Colonel Roosevelt; and when a red-necked colonel without corsets came to demand our surrender on about a hundred criminal counts, the secretary received him alone in a small room and contrived to satisfy him somehow.

The long and the short of it was that Miss Eliot was permitted to continue her journey to Switzerland, which she subsequently did, leaving Jeremy disconsolate for fifteen minutes and the story to progress without her. I have never seen her since, although I have been told that she described me when she got home as a "great, dark lunatic, who might have got her into jail if it hadn't been for the handsome Mr. Jeremy Ross." But she never saw him again either, so no harm was done.

Jeremy and I were ordered to leave Germany that night, under embassy escort as far as the frontier — for which we had to pay. We didn't mind that much, since business with the *vons* and *zus* looked stagnant. We were also forbidden to return for twelve months, and forbidden even after that lapse of time without a special police permit. But as neither of us ever wanted to go back, that hardly mattered.

We had supper at the embassy, and Jeremy passed the time with conjuring tricks and ventriloquism, giving a performance with hardly any paraphernalia that would have passed muster on any stage in the world. He could do stunts with billiard balls, and make a Japanese mask talk in a way that brought to mind those ever-green romances about Indian fakirs. In fact, I don't think it would have surprized anybody much when it was time for us to start for the train, if he had performed the fabled trick of throwing up a rope into the air, climbing up it out of sight, and pulling the rope after him.

The only thing that could surprise you about Jeremy Ross after you had known him for an hour or two would be to see him gloomy or depressed, or at a loss for some unusual way of passing time.

All the way to the Dutch frontier he kept the embassy escort and the train crew amused with sleight-of-hand tricks, banter, and ventriloquism. Perhaps his best stunt was making a fat man, who had a corner seat in our compartment say outrageous things about the Kaiser in his sleep. When he tired of that he spilled a flow of reminiscences that could not have been lies, because no man could have invented all that much.

He seemed to have worked at every trade there is, and to have forgotten nothing. Youngest son of a well-to-do ranch-owner, he had rebelled at the station routine and set out to make his own fortune at the age of fourteen. When I met him in Berlin he was twenty-three or four, and though the fortune hadn't taken shape yet he seemed to have enough to get along with and was certainly well equipped with experience.

WHEN WE LEFT the train in Holland the conductor, the ticket-man and several passengers, including the fat one who had been made to say things in his sleep, insisted on shaking hands. It was a miserable little junction station, but that did not disturb Jeremy; as soon as the farewells were over and we had seen the embassy fellow into the return train for Berlin he took my arm and proposed that we should set out at once to explore Holland.

But I demurred. I couldn't afford in those days to wander at large — or thought I couldn't, which comes to about the same thing.

"Something'll turn up. It always does," he prophesied. "Dutch money's all right; you can spend it. It's round and it rolls. Let's get some."

But I hadn't yet learned the difference between being timorous and being cautious. I quoted the old jingle that has somehow lasted down the years as a label for the *Meinheers* —

> *"In matters of commerce the fault of the Dutch*
> *Lies in giving too little and asking too much."*

"All right," he answered. "Come with me to Australia. Let's try West Aus. Get some camels and find gold in the desert. Great game. Make a pile quick and settle down to a life of roving. Come on!"

I wonder what it is that makes a man deliberately decide against his inclination. There wasn't really any reason why I shouldn't go with Jeremy. A merrier companion couldn't be, or a braver. He would get into trouble, of course, but chuckle his way out of it; and you don't mind sharing any sort of difficulty with a mate who is game to lift his end of it. His optimism and my comparative caution might have made us good partners.

But I had London in mind and a brace of millionaires whose profitable passion is to finance such folk as me, and Jeremy wouldn't try London on any terms.

"Dukes, knights, lords, earls — afternoon tea in the office — wipe your feet on the mat, please — one of the Empire's splendid sons when dividends ain't rolling in and the bankers want a war — blooming Botany Bay Colonial when the fighting's over! No, I've seen London. The king may have it! I wouldn't fight for the Empire again, not if they offered to give me the whole damn thing for my trouble!"

He spent the best part of two days trying to lure me to Australia, recounting the delights of "humping bluey," the romantic possibilities of pearling on shares, the carefree existence that a man might live trading cattle on the long drive down from the northern territories, and the fortunes to be made by "paddocking" in West Aus.

But that something — maybe intuition — that so many people offer to explain and no man understands, urged me elsewhere. I offered to share up with Jeremy whatever arrangement I could contrive with the men in London; but the notion seemed to be fixed in his head that making profits for any one outside Australia was treason. I don't say he wasn't right. Nobody ever made it clear to me why international financiers should be allowed to weave empires on a basis of percentages for the fellows who do the work. But Jeremy couldn't, or wouldn't see a difference that looks clear to me between grub-staking a man on shares and criminal plutocracy. He said there was no such thing as fair play in financial circles outside Australia, and not even too much of it there.

Not that he was a socialist, or a communist, or any other kind of reformer. He could sum up his philosophy and politics in about ten words: "If there's gold in a stream, and I can pan it, what in Hell do I need a financier for? I'm the young feller that's going to finance any operations I'm engaged in."

I asked him what he proposed to do when he had made the pile he talked of hopefully; how would he invest it?

"I won't," he said, "I'll spend it. You wait and see!"

I don't carry my craving for independence all that far. I've made my little pile, and used the money of more than one financier to do it. The dollars are salted down in United States Government securities, and I figure now that the world will have to go to pieces before any man can crowd me to the wall. I'll tell you what happened to Jeremy presently; and although my method has worked so well for me, I'm still not sure that his hasn't suited him equally well. It's a matter of individuality, each man to his own affairs, of which there is a lot too little nowadays.

I said good-by to Jeremy in Rotterdam, where he took passage for Australia, glorying rebelliously in the steamer's foreign registry. He swore over the taffrail — I was going to say solemnly, but he never did anything that way — at the top of his lungs, at all events, that he would never sail again under the British flag, salute another British officer, set foot in England, or pay taxes. He also gave me a specific message to deliver to the king, wished me well rid of my financiers, and begged me to get religion and come to Australia "where God rides horseback."

The last I saw of him on that occasion he was performing on the bridge deck as the steamer swung into the tide, juggling with three opened, but not empty, beer bottles and as many tumblers, dancing to his own tune simultaneously. And the tune that he whistled was as free from care or any real malice as his own heart.

For a day or two I missed him sorely and wished I had gone with him. Then, as such things do happen in this rapid motion-picture world, he passed from mind in a new welter of business negotiations. My twin millionaires saw a chance in the prospect that I offered them; we signed up, and I went to Abyssinia, where I was able to pack up a decent competence and return them several hundred per cent on their outlay; which may be immoral, but is something I peculiarly like to do.

What with digging gold, and hunting elephants on the side, I don't believe I thought of Jeremy Ross more than once or twice during all the time I stayed in Abyssinia, a land whose riches are kept idle under a blanket of graft that gives you all you need to occupy your mind.

Chapter II

"Grim's a bird — you ought to meet Grim."

NOW SKIP A NUMBER of years. The end of 1913 found me still in Abyssinia endeavoring with varying success to protect my financiers' investment. But in January, 1916, I got out at last and headed down the Nile for Cairo, where, after a deal of arguing, the military let me have a room at one of the two big hotels.

Some of you don't need telling what those places were like in war-time. The Mount Nelson in Cape Town during the Boer War was a kindergarten to it. The notice at the front door, "Out of Bounds to all Enlisted Men," summed up the situation. You couldn't breathe for brass hats, or do a thing without being told you mustn't; and all the things you mustn't do were being done right and left by every one who had a relative at the War Office or a good-looking wife who entertained.

I tried for a while to horn in somewhere and be useful; but you couldn't get near Allenby or Lawrence or any man who was really responsible. The rest were willing to have you know that the ground whereon they stood was holy; in fact, you had to concede that point before they'd talk to you at all. Thereafter, whatever you wanted to know was an official secret, but you were usually allowed to pay for drinks.

It petered down finally to the alternative of going home, or taking a hand along with the Levantines in profiteer contracts for army supplies, which is a trade I don't take to readily. So I decided it wasn't my war, put my name down on the waiting list for a passage to the States, and waited. There are worse places to wait in, once you're definitely a spectator and don't care who cheats whom, or why. And while I waited I ran into Jeremy Ross again.

It was no surprize to see him once more in British uniform. Peter the Apostle set the example of protesting and then swallowing the protest. Jeremy erred in first-class company, and appeared to thrive on it. But he was sinning, too, against the army regulations, which is much worse, as well as likelier to bring instant punishment. Within ten paces of that notice by the hotel door, directly facing it, he, Jeremy Ross, a sergeant with the worsted chevrons on his sleeve, sat drinking whisky-and-soda at a table between two palms on the front veranda, in full view of any righteous personage who might pass.

It was scandalous, outrageous, subversive of all social order — more dangerous, I dare say, than trading with the enemy or spying for the other side. So I went and sat down on the chair in front of him, and ordered the Nubian waiter to charge the drinks to me, having a notion in the back of my head that for the second time I was going to steer Jeremy out of a scrape.

Well, glad to see me was no word for it. Some men blaze out like the sun from behind a cloud when they meet a friend, and Jeremy was one of them. He couldn't have made more noise if he had struck it lucky in the gold-fields of West Australia, where men don't celebrate in whispers; and he tried to tell me all his adventures since we parted in one long sentence. But he couldn't crowd it in or talk sense for high spirits.

He was perfectly sober and looked handsomer than ever in his broad-brimmed felt hat with the black cock's feather; moreover, he was as full as usual of disrespect for possible consequences and bubbling with amusement at the discomfort of one or two officers not far away, whose business it didn't happen to be to substitute for the provost marshal. They were as indignant as ruffled turkey-cocks, and I remarked on it.

"On edge, ain't they," laughed Jeremy. "But we Australians have made a bit of a rep for ourselves. You'll notice none of them'll interfere until somebody comes who's big enough to give them Hell for letting dirt like me sit in the sight of nabobs. Crikey! I could tell you tales about what's happened up there in Palestine when the staff tried to what they call discipline us chaps that would make you gasp. We've done most of the hard fighting; that's all right; that's what we're here for. But they haven't got us feeding out of their jeweled hands exactly. Listen to this."

And he told me tale after tale that never got into the papers about how the Australians had left their mark on the General Staff as well as on the Turks and Germans. Maybe he exaggerated, but I dare say not. I know what those fellows did and did not do in South Africa, and there were more of them on this occasion, farther from home and possessed of even less respect than formerly for swank, eye-wash, and petty tyranny.

The inevitable happened at the end of half an hour. A staff-major came out of the hotel, who thought more of the line between enlistment and commission than of that great gulf reported to be fixed between heaven and the other place. He marched straight up and demanded to know what Jeremy thought he was doing there.

"He's my guest," I answered, before Jeremy could get a word in. "You can find out, if you care to, that whatever he has had to drink is charged to me."

But all that did was to include me in the class of undesirables. I was told I had sinned more grievously than Jeremy, and that I would be turned out of the hotel if I didn't mend my ways. He demanded my name. I offered to exchange cards, which he refused; so I advised him to mend his manners, if he thought that could be done without any risk to his health, and he went off in a towering rage in search of the provost marshal.

I was fully determined by that time to stick it out and see the affair through with Jeremy. It wouldn't have been the slightest use for either of us to clear out, for there was a provost sergeant watching us from over the way, who would simply have arrested Jeremy out of hand. I suppose the only reason why the staff-major hadn't ordered him to do that anyhow was his ambition to include me in the picnic, and any one less than a full-blown marshal with the correct stars on his shoulder and the proper badge might shake down a windfall of enforced apologies, and all that disagreeable kind of thing, for an assault on an American civilian.

And Jeremy was simply in his element. It was a long time before the provost marshal came, and he passed it calling full attention to his crime, laughing, chuckling, cracking jokes, and describing for my benefit the comforts of the desert bull-pen out by the Pyramids, where he assured me I should be locked up along with him.

Then came one of those dusky magicians who produce day-old chickens out of a tarboosh on hotel verandas, and we watched him for about ten minutes, until Jeremy grew scornful of such amateurish stunts and elected to give the fellow a lesson. But it wasn't all professional pride; he wanted, too, to show me what a mastery he had of Arabic, which he must have learned in about a year in between terrific bouts of fighting.

"Picked it up, haven't I?" he said over his shoulder between one superb trick and the next. There were officers all around us now, ignoring military caste for the sake of being mystified. A sub-altern brought the pool balls from the billiard table, and Jeremy made them crawl all over his arms as if they were bewitched; the Egyptian was pushed into the background, and slunk away disgruntled.

An officer came along with a fox-terrier; Jeremy took the dog on his knee — he has a way with animals that makes them instant friends and turned on his ventriloquism, making the pup give Arabic answers to his remarks in English.

"Wish Grim was here," he said to me when he paused to swallow a drink and light a cigaret.

"Who's Grim?"

"One of you Yanks. First-class fellow. Working under Lawrence over in Arabia. I tried to get a transfer to his show damned free and easy — independent — no airs — just the kind of job I like. Grim was willing, but nothing came of it; some brass hat got jealous, I suppose; nobody loves an Australian. If Grim was here now I'd show him a thing or two. He'd apply for me quick, and have his own way about it. Grim's a bird — quiet chap nearly all the time, but game to tell a full-blown general to go to as soon as look at him. You ought to meet Grim. Watch this."

But watching him was no use; you couldn't tell how he did it. He spun twenty coins of different sizes on the table and palmed the lot with one swipe of his hand. You could hear them click into place on top of one another, but half a second later when he opened his hand it was empty. It looked logical and easy after that when he produced them, with his other hand, out of the pup's mouth.

Then came the provost marshal, whose profession is to spoil sport and put the lid on entertainment. He had been brought away from an afternoon bridge-party, and was in a corresponding frame of mind — didn't know me — didn't want to know me — hadn't time to listen to me — ordered Jeremy under arrest at once — and threatened to arrest me in the bargain if I had any more to say.

So I saw a way to help Jeremy once more out of a military entanglement and said a great deal fervently. But I was careful what I said and the provost marshal wasn't. An officer in uniform, who has the law and regulations on his side, simply can't afford to be abusive to a civilian who isn't scared. There never was a military regulation yet devised that couldn't be off-set somehow, as the Belgians proved to Von Bissing.

He did exactly what I hoped he would do in the end — ordered me put out of the hotel, added one or two remarks about my nationality, called me a slacker because I wasn't in uniform, and strode away fuming.

Meanwhile, Jeremy had been marched off in disgrace, even so looking not at all dejected. His black cock's feather danced along jauntily; and even the provost sergeant couldn't keep the guard from laughing at his jokes.

"Try your Embassy again!" he shouted to me from the street.

But the U.S. doesn't keep an embassy in Cairo, and a consul-general has his limitations; our consul might have made it all right for me, but couldn't help Jeremy. Bankers are the boys, when they're your friends; and you can't live several years in Abyssinia, making money for other people, without being on good terms with a Cairo banker.

There was a man of millions, whose head office was in London, who had instructions from my financial twins to do anything he could for me at any time. I found him in his office, and the rest was easy, although it did take a day or two. He sent for my effects from the hotel and put me up in his private house at Ramleh, pending a settlement.

There was nothing that I wanted — not even an apology. The provost marshal hadn't gone an inch beyond his rights in having me turned out of the hotel; and as for bad language, I'm no school-girl; I've listened to a lot of it, and used some too. But — well, you know the difference between men, whose troubles are their own affair and serve 'em right, and the other sort, whose part you'll take whether they deserve punishment or not? I'd have stood by Jeremy if he'd committed murder.

The solution was all the easier because my banker acquaintance had social notions and didn't like that provost marshal's manners; and you may believe it or not, but when a war is on, and the army, and army contractors need money every day, he who deals in cash across the counter has more influence than any ten ambassadors.

THREE DAYS AFTER the incident I went down, armed with an official pass, to the Australian camp near the Pyramids to see Jeremy, and found him in a barbed-wire enclosure in the hot sun digging a nice square hole in the sand under the eyes of a sergeant-major.

They had reduced him to the ranks for absence without leave, but weren't content with that. A theory was being tried just then that drasticism was the only physic for Australians; so, for having dared to sit and drink in a hotel reserved for the higher caste, he was sentenced to dig ten holes, each to be exactly ten feet square and ten deep, in yielding sand and afterward fill them up again. He was still in the first hole when I found him; and because my pass expressly stated that I might talk to him alone the sergeant-major had to withdraw out of earshot.

Jeremy didn't say much at first. He smoothed the side of the hole with his shovel, grinned at me, patted another rough place, and presently expressed his judgment of the British Empire.

"I hope the Hottentots get London," he said. "I'd like to see an army of our Australian Aborigines looting the Bank of England. And the thing to do with the Royal Family is to put 'em in cages and send 'em on tour with the circus. The fall of Rome was a penny squib to what I hope happens to England, and I'd help any one except the Kaiser who had sense enough to take a crack at it. No use helping the Kaiser; he hasn't got guts; besides, if he won, he'd be worse, supposing that's possible. But to think I volunteered — just think of it! Me that belonged to the regiment that won the Boer War and took oath to see the whole British Empire into Hell before we'd ever fight for that crowd again! But what's the use of talking? Wait till I get out of uniform, and see. That's all!"

I helped him out of the hole, gave him cigarets, and we sat down on the sand together, facing.

"How about that fellow Grim you told me about?" said I. "Would you care to join him?"

"Wouldn't I! Grim is for Feisul, and so am I. But it can't be done. They keep Australians for the fighting and fatigues. They're using Feisul the same way — ditch him soon as the war's won — wait and see."

"I can't get your rank restored," I said.

"Don't try," he answered. "I'd stuff the chevrons down the throat of the first British officer I met!"

"But I know a man who can get you transferred to Akaba under Grim," I went on.

"Then you're my enemy!"

"How so?"

"For not having done it already."

So I got his promise not to fall foul of any regulations, nor of any man — not even a sergeant-major until he should set foot in Arabia; and with that understanding I returned to my banker, who by that time had set three club committees by the ears and had cabled London and the U.S.A. Financiers don't stop short of taking pains when they pursue vendettas.

The cables weren't working very well, and it was another week — Jeremy had dug more than half his holes — before the General Staff began to realize my nuisance value. I received an official call from a major, who knew nothing of what had taken place, but supposed he could straighten the matter out over a couple of cigars.

He began by saying he thought it very decent of me not to have complained to the consul-general.

But I followed the banker's instructions carefully and the major left with the impression that the least I wanted was the degradation of the provost marshal to the ranks, together with personal apologies from all concerned to almost everybody in America. The banker, who was present during the interview, dropped hints at intervals about my financial connections.

The General Staff was busy and worried, and in no mood to pause in its stride for the sake of a provost marshal's dignity. Somebody higher up told him sharply that he must straighten the tangle out himself at once, or take the consequences; so he took the only course left to him and sent one of his assistants to ask for an appointment for his chief.

On the banker's advice, I wasn't in. But the door was open between the two rooms; the banker did the talking and I listened. "You know what these Americans are — pig-headed men. Once they're set on a course they're hard to turn. This man is a pretty good fellow, but he's no man's fool to be pacified with a perfunctory apology."

"What does he want, then? Does he expect the provost to walk here on foot with peas in his boots and call out *Peccavi* through the back door? He's crazy if he expects a man like Colonel Gootch to come and grovel to him."

"I don't think it would amuse him in the least to see anybody grovel."

"Well, what does he want?"

"An apology, of course. He was publicly insulted; he's entitled to an apology in public, and as a guest in my house I'd expect him to demand at least that. But he wants more. As a practical man he demands some practical proof of regret and of willingness to make amends."

"Good Lord! You mean money?"

"Of course I don't, nor does he. You know better than that. At the time of the insult he had an Australian with him — Sergeant Jeremy Ross by name — an old friend whom he'd met that afternoon for the first time in ten years. It seems the Australian was the cause of all the trouble — out of bounds at my friend's invitation in a place reserved for officers. The Australian was very severely punished as well as reduced to the ranks, and my friend feels badly about it."

"Good God! D'you mean he expects Gootch to go and kiss the sergeant on both cheeks and beg his pardon?"

"Hardly But you may tell Provost Marshal Gootch privately from me that if he cared to arrange that Australian's transfer to Akaba for special duty under Captain Grim, there's no doubt I could persuade my friend to accept an apology in this room and let the whole matter drop."

"But Colonel Gootch hasn't anything to do with transfers."

"He has influence. Let him use it. You'd better make it clear to Colonel Gootch that he'll have me to deal with unless he does the right thing pretty quickly. I have business at headquarters tomorrow noon. It might be best for all concerned if I could say at that time that the air is clear again. I've heard of bigger men than Gootch being transferred to less agreeable duties."

"Well, I'll tell him."

"Put it bluntly. will you? Tell him you talked with me."

Gootch understood the situation and got busy. Napoleon may have told the truth about the British in that famous remark of his; maybe he spoke collectively; but I can certify that one high-handed colonel, at all events, knew when he was beaten. Jeremy was excused from digging holes that afternoon, and his transfer to Akaba was arranged the same evening.

The apology to me, too, left nothing to be desired; it began by being stiff and throaty, but ended in armchairs with whisky-and-soda. In fact, I rather think Gootch and I were on good terms before he left: it was his suggestion that I might like to travel with Jeremy as far as Port Said, and he provided me a pass that came pretty near to being the key of Egypt.

So I traveled in a troop-train through a hot night, listening to Jeremy's accounts of what had happened to him in the years between. It seemed he had even been a police-court magistrate, and had done almost everything else from trading horses down to conjuring in small towns with a traveling vaudeville troupe.

But he thought that none of the things that he had done were half as inexplicably marvelous as my getting him that transfer for special duty under James Schuyler Grim the American, and he swore friendship forever on the strength of it.

This time he waved good-by with his cock's-plume hat from the deck of a decrepit tug in the Suez Canal, and his last words were of jubilantly roared advice to me to get attached to Grim's command in some way.

"Grim's the real thing," he shouted. "Come along and see life!"

At the last glimpse I had he was dancing on the tug's poop, laughing and making friends with every one on board. He had promised to write, but of course he didn't, and the letters I wrote to him were all returned eventually marked "undelivered for reason stated." The fact that the reason wasn't stated hardly shed much light on Jeremy's career.

However, I received news of him almost simultaneously with those undelivered but carefully censored returned letters of mine. My banker friend in Cairo wrote to me after I got back to the States, enclosing a clipping from an official list of casualties. It read:

> **Trooper Jeremy Wallace Ross.**
> **—th Australian Light Horse.**
> **On special duty Akaba. Missing.**

I wrote in vain for further details. Nothing seemed to be known about him, and although the authorities were courteous and apparently took great pains to find out for me, "presumably dead" was the final official verdict. So I wished I hadn't engineered his transfer to Akaba, and more or less forgot him once again.

Chapter III

"Protection looks best from a long way off."

NOW SKIP SEVERAL more years. Mastery of time and space is the prerogative of him who tells tales. and possibly has something to do with the reader's contentment. In what is called real life the days are steps of a tedious stair, up which we climb unhandily enough with never a chance to take ten dozen in a stride during the monotonous interludes when nothing seems to happen. Even when we fall instead of climbing we must bump down one day at a time, with the bottom everlastingly receding as discomfort grows. For nothing I ever read, or heard, or saw convinced me that there is top or bottom; we just go on forever, either way, one step at a time.

But in a story you can leave out the uninteresting parts, and omit mention of the people who crowd the steps uncomfortably. The whole world's history, and the gamut of human cussedness go to the making of every incident and give biologists a deal of material to keep them busy. But we, who for our peace of mind are not biologists or dry-as-dust historians, may sum up every situation in five monosyllables: *So it came to pass.*

It came to pass, then, that in 1920 I was back in the Near East — in Jerusalem, to be exact — not at a loose end, nor on a lost trail, but venturing more or less at random for an opportunity. Being independent and in the prime of life — which is the present moment in which every healthy fellow finds himself and has nothing to do with middle age — I was in position to engage in any pursuit that interested me.

I like to see the fruit of my labor in the form of invested dollars. I think a man is a fool who doesn't salt down more than half of what he earns; but no man is entitled to an opinion who lacks the courage of it. I've been called more than my share of hard names by men who describe themselves as generous, but I shan't have to tax their generosity when old age comes, because I have made it a rule to reckon costs up in advance and never to engage in anything until I can see which side the bread is buttered on. You might call me a cautious man, and in one sense conservative.

Nevertheless, I have had my full share of fun and look forward to plenty more; and the reason of that is as simple as addition. I have never looked for money merely for the sake of getting money. The game has got to interest me first; and I've discovered this: That when you're really interested you can start a good game anywhere. The fact that you are interested opens doors.

So, although Jerusalem looks at the first glance like a strange choice for a professional prospector as a jumping-off-place into the unknown; and although it certainly would be the worst place imaginable for a man dependent on his earnings from month to month, with its prodigious interest as a maelstrom of human emotions fixed in the centre of the habitable surface of the world, within a day's ride of the unknown in more than one direction, it suited my case perfectly.

Where all the tribes, all the politics, most of the creeds and a generous sprinkling of cranks foregather, there the tales blow like blossom in the wind. Blossom that sticks begets fruit; every blown blossom had to have a tree to grow on, and you can find the tree if you look long enough. In other words, most tales are worth investigating for the truth that underlies them; and if you want one tale a minute, each wilder than the last, just try Jerusalem for a month or so.

And as I have already told, it was in Jerusalem that I at last met the James Schuyler Grim who Jeremy had said was such a first-class fellow. Lawrence, who did more than any living man to defeat the Turks, by composing Arab differences and swinging the Arabs into line behind Feisul to fight on Allenby's right wing, had returned to England long ago. Most of the quiet handful who achieved impossibilities for Lawrence's sake had followed him into retirement or scattered over the earth to new fields of activity. But Grim stayed on in the Intelligence Department, and I have told several adventures that I had with him.

Grim isn't a man whom you would normally expect to lead you on to fortune — nor to fame; for he appears to find his meagre pay sufficient, and isn't even keen enough on that to cling to his job unless the British let him have his own way. And publicity offends him like a bad smell. He had to know me intimately for months, and I had to make him all kinds of promises, before he gave me permission to lay bare some of his doings.

And I don't mean by that that he is modest in the usual meaning of the word; for he isn't. He knows his own value and pits himself with confidence against odds and in situations that would make his seniors in the service gasp. But he is a man of one idea; and as well as I can describe it in a sentence it consists in using his own extraordinary ability to the utmost. What he knows is Arabia, Syria, Egypt, and Arabs.

What he can do is to understand the Arab and bring out his good qualities. What he thinks is that Feisul, third son of the King of Mecca, who — for the first time since Saladin — united the Arabs under one banner in one cause, should be allowed to work out some form of independent Arab government. What he does is to devote his whole energy along that line, making use of his commission in the British army because it gives him authority and funds.

Mind you, he earns the money that the British pay him; and, seeing that he is an American, with no real claim to their consideration since peace was signed, it isn't likely they would continue him in the service unless they were sure they had their money's worth. I found him as Jeremy described, a man "game at any time to tell a full-blown general to go to Hell," and the convenience must therefore be considered mutual; the British pay Grim because he is useful to them; he accepts their pay, and wears their uniform at times, because that is the line of least resistance to the furtherance of the cause he has at heart.

Most people like him, although some officials are jealous of his ability and of the scope that he enjoys in consequence; for he goes just where and when he chooses as a rule, which makes his lot considerably pleasanter than that of the routine men tied down to stuffy quarters in Jerusalem, Nablus, Haifa, and such posts.

Most criminals like him, for though he frustrates their more important schemes with an ingenuity that must seem almost supernatural to them, he is never vindictive. The crowded jail in Jerusalem is full of Grim's friends; and the toughest rogues of the Near East are his best assistants, for if ever a man took others as he found them, discovered the best in each, and bent it to the cause he has espoused, that man is Grim.

I remember how in my callow days I couldn't sit down at ease with men possessed of a different notion of morality from mine. Nowadays, on the rare occasions when I lie awake, I spend the time laughing at the superior airs of that aspiring young moralist who once on a time was me. Contact with the earth's ends soon kicks out of you, of course, ninety per cent. of your puppyhood but a modicum remains that varies with the individual, and it needed Grim to teach me that a murderer, for instance, isn't necessarily a bit worse than a politician, nor either of them so much worse than you and me that you could measure the difference with a micrometer.

In Grim's company I have spent days in the intimate society of professional thieves, to whom murder was a side-line of the business, and I reckon I'm the better for it; for Grim has the faculty of bringing out what makes the world such an amazing place — the infinite capacity possessed by every rascal for doing the decent thing deliberately.

Haven't you seen men who can take ill-broken horses and drive them all day long without a kick or an accident, because of sympathy and understanding without a weak spot in it? That best describes Grim's way. There isn't any mush in him. Slushy sentiment won't manage men when a crisis comes any more than petting will control stampeding cattle.

He looks facts in the face without wincing, and where whip, rein, and voice are called for he can use them; but, though I have been in more than a score of uncommonly tight places along with Grim, I have never once heard him make an ill-considered threat, or seen him weak for a second when firmness was the cue. The truth is, he can read the hearts of men, which is the only book worth reading in the long run, although there are some printed ones that help you to understand; it is full from end to end of unexpected wonders, and those cynics who assert that man's nature is predominantly evil are ignorant fools, who lie.

And, as I have said, Grim hates publicity. He even hates to air his views, or to discuss information before the minute comes for using it. That makes him a rather disconcerting man to get along with, for he springs things on you when you least expect, and keeps you in the dark at times when you would give ten years of your life for the certainty of living ten more minutes. I think he is obsessed by the unusual belief that to share his thoughts lessens their fertility, and I know he regards all propaganda as a foolish and indecent waste of time.

So the mere fact that he doesn't answer, or shakes his head, or looks bored, or says he doesn't know, doesn't prove much. I remember asking him, not long after I first met him in Jerusalem, for some account of Jeremy's doings in Arabia and of how the merry fellow lost the number of his mess.

To my surprize Grim denied all knowledge of him, although not by any means convincingly. He didn't seem to try to be convincing. He looked up from the book he was reading and stared at me for about thirty seconds with those baffling eyes of his that now and then gleam so brilliantly under the bushy eyebrows that they almost seem on fire. He had been smiling at something he had just read, but now his lips set noncommittally in a straight line.

"Why? What do you know of him?" he asked.

It struck me at once as improbable that Jeremy had never mentioned me to Grim, seeing that I had been instrumental in bringing the two together in Akaba. However, it isn't always good manners to make a display of incredulity; and there isn't a set of circumstances anywhere, nor ever was, in which bad manners are less than a mistake. So I took the question at its face value and told all I knew about Jeremy from the beginning.

Grim closed his book and listened with apparently deep interest, never interrupting once. Not one least gesture betrayed previous knowledge of the Australian; and although he smiled once or twice at the accounts of Jeremy's misdeeds, it wasn't with any air of being familiar with them. All the same, I still wasn't convinced.

"I can't tell you a thing about him," he said at last, when I had come to the end of my tale and waited for Grim to make a remark of some sort. Then he resumed his reading, holding the book so that I could no longer see his face, which may have been an accident but left me less convinced than ever.

I formed the conclusion that my friend Jeremy Ross must have done something discreditable, which Grim preferred to leave undiscussed, that it might be forgotten the sooner. Strange, isn't it, how we jump to the worst conclusions and associate all silence with unpleasantness? Since that was my judgment of the situation, decency obliged me to keep silence too — that and a discreditable, although not unique desire to dissociate myself from the record of a man who appeared to have failed in the last pinch. That's another strange thing, isn't it, how decency and despicable motives run in double harness!

There were plenty of incidents after that, when I ventured with Grim and his following of born thieves into the trans-Jordan country, which brought Jeremy to mind again; but I kept my thoughts to myself and never once referred to him.

Nevertheless, the more I learned of the amazing story of what Lawrence and his handful did in the war, with another handful of untrumpeted zealots toiling in their rear, the less I liked to remain ignorant of Jeremy's share in the doings. And the more I turned over in mind what I did know of Jeremy, the less probable it seemed that what I did not know could be much to his discredit.

Wild he was certainly, and free with his opinions about men and circumstances that he did not like; but it seemed increasingly incredible that Jeremy, wearing the uniform of a free man who had volunteered for foreign service, would do anything meriting the name of treason.

In my experience, free-speaking men of courage are less likely to betray their flag than are some of the patrioteers, who wave their hats in air when the flag goes by, but would sell it, and throw their country in, for less than Esau took in exchange for his birthright.

Neither was Jeremy Ross a likely plunderer. There are loose-ended men, of course, who constitutionally can't let alone such opportunities for pouching money as unguarded army supplies provide. But Jeremy was one of those fellows who could make money easily without stooping to dishonesty. In fact, it was bellicose honesty in harness with boisterous humor that made him rail at shams and got him so often into trouble. That kind of fellow doesn't steal.

The only plausible supposition left, then, was the oldest in the world. Jeremy was a handsome man with a little dark mustache that turned naturally upward and made you think of d'Artagnan. He had eyes and a smile, free shoulders and a horseman's supple loins, that together with his bubbling spirits might easily have stirred the ambition of a desert-born Delilah.

There are women in all lands who are like spiders, not content to play the vampire game, but only satisfied when they have lured, bled white and finally destroyed. Moslem countries are the last in which a wise man would run that kind of risk; but Jeremy Ross — clever, brilliant, alert, courageous — was not nearly always wise. A woman seemed the likeliest guess; but that only added to my desire to learn all the facts.

Patience, however, is my long suit. I have had to acquire that quality, for lack of some of those more marketable talents with which men born under other stars than mine seem to attain to what they want so easily. I take it that patience had quite a lot to do with Grim's selection of me to go with him on expeditions, for

I have no strategic or diplomatic genius. True, he had my services for nothing, and that is quite a consideration when you remember how poor the governments are in these days, so that all the unspectacular, unpopular departments must have their expense sheets pared to the bone.

It is also true that hard knocks and harder work in all kinds of out-of-the-way places have made me in a sort of way dependable. I have been let down too badly and too often by men who called themselves assistants, to care to submit another fellow to that sort of mortification.

I can talk Hindustani pretty well, and my skin has been burned a sort of raw mahogany color by sun and wind and sea, which makes it comparatively easy for me to pose as an Indian Moslem in places where Indians are well known by repute but rather rare. And I have learned enough Arabic to understand the drift of things, and to hold up my end in any argument.

But Grim, who can act the part of an Arab so perfectly as to deceive the most suspicious of them — and there isn't a more swiftly suspicious race under heaven — could have found dozens of men who understood the Arabs better, and who could disguise themselves and act their parts better than I.

Grim is really a long-headed imaginative business man in a peculiar environment. Even in his major's uniform he looks the part. In civilian clothes you couldn't possibly mistake him. He is one of those men for whom the Napoleons of commerce hunt ceaselessly, and to whom, when discovered, they pay whatever salary the find considers himself worth.

For make no mistake about it, nine-tenths of the art of making millions lies in knowing a born executive when you see him in the raw. And again, nine-tenths of an executive's worth consists in knowing men. Grim knows all about men. He has a genius for judging just how far a given individual will go in certain circumstances. He understands how far to trust, and just when to mistrust.

And, greatest art of all, he knows how to cajole a notoriously dishonest fellow into playing straight, as well as how to forestall the vastly more difficult customers who practise knavery under the cloak of a good reputation.

So I claim it is a feather in my cap that Grim made a friend of me, and invited me to share his quarters in Jerusalem in the funny little stone house down an alley at the back of the Zionist hospital. As his friend I must count myself among a score or two of cut-throats, some of whom are in the jail this minute, and two of whom they tell me are now under sentence to be hanged.

But I don't find the association unendurable. In fact, the meannesses of what is called polite society, where men and women commit their crimes by proxy, bore me rather soon, and I'm minded to go back and meet some of those honest thieves and murderers again. I like things and people labeled with their proper names.

We didn't use Grim's quarters for many days on end, for the Administration wasn't paying him to sit down and grow fat. One expedition followed another with the swiftness and almost the regularity of a motion-picture serial, and between times, when Grim wasn't reading, there was a constant succession of visitors, who brought in scraps of information from zones not reached by rail or telegraph.

We had almost daily news of Mustapha Kemal in Anatolia. Now and then there were tales of the Bolsheviki in northern Persia, and once when I was present a hairy, swarthy, smelly fellow brought information from as far away as Samarkand. The spies who reported at headquarters on the Mount of Olives were usually sent along to Grim to repeat their story to him personally, so that before you had been in his company a week you felt as if you were posted in the center of a great map, with all the roads, tracks, wires, and rivers radiating outward from you.

Few of the visitors knew how to behave in so-called civilized surroundings, and most of them when offered a seat preferred a mat or a cushion on the floor. Your progressive Arab likes to air what he thinks are occidental manners, but the men familiar with deserts can't disgorge their news unless you let them sit at ease in their accustomed way.

By constant repetition one peculiarity became remarkable — the farther away the place from which any of our visitors came, the more insistent that man would be that Grim should return with him to help straighten matters out.

I don't think that meant that Grim's fame had reached all the way to Samarkand, for instance. His Arab name, Jimgrim, can be conjured with throughout northern Arabia and Syria, but hardly beyond that; and at any rate he put a totally different construction on the circumstance.

"You see?" he laughed one afternoon. "When they're not familiar with western methods and only know of them by hearsay, they're crazy to call us in. But the folk near by, who've had a dose or two of our enlightenment, would rather be let alone in future. Notice it? The stories from fifty or a hundred miles away are mostly given one kind of twist calculated to calm the Administration's nerves; from beyond that the twist is exactly reversed. European protection looks best from a long way off. Well, I'm dead set against outside interference. If I could have my way, there'd be no meddling in foreign lands. Each to his own affairs is my creed."

But, like the rest of us, Grim can't have his own way very often and has to be content with compromise.

ONE AFTERNOON, about a month after our return from the affair with Ali Higg at Petra, there came a man on camel-back, followed and noisily rebuked by a couple of mounted policemen, who insisted that he should report himself and his business first at police headquarters.

But he had no use for the police, and was much too wise to stop and argue, or to draw his weapons and give them an excuse to call assistance and arrest him. He knew the way to Grim's quarters and sent his camel along at top speed, stone-deaf to shouts, threats, commands, and all abuse.

He dismounted at the narrow stone gateway without making his camel kneel, and leaving the beast for the police to watch strode straight in unannounced, brushing aside the servant who ran to the door to question him.

Grim and I happened to be playing chess, with the board between us on a stool in front of the fireplace. The man stood watching us in silence for two or three minutes, patient now that he had reached his goal; and Grim didn't appear to notice him, although the smell of human and camel sweat blended and the fellow's heavy breathing were remarkable, to state it mildly.

It was five minutes before the Arab saw fit to interrupt.

"*Salaam aleikum, ya* Jimgrim!" he said at last. "That game you play there is a slow one. I have brought you word across the desert of a swift one that a man must play between life and death. Ben Saoud summons you!"

Chapter IV

"In the name of Him Who never sleeps it is a bargain!"

OUR VISITOR WAS TALL as well as smelly, and he smelt of other things besides sweat — the desert, for instance, which, like the salt sea, has its own aroma. It makes some folk afraid before they are conscious of what frightens them, filling others with a vague restlessness.

All smells are certainly to be included in that new elusive law of relativity. Grim and I, freshly tubbed, in a clean-swept room, were more offensive to that Bedouin than he to us. He had cotton stuffed in his nostrils, an habitual indignity the desert people offer to the cities on the rare occasions when they leave behind the safety of all outdoors and contemptuously tread the peril-haunted streets.

There was nothing about our quarters that he enjoyed. He stood with his big brown eyes wide open, not distrustful, for he knew Grim, but about as alert as a horse just in off the range, turning his head an inch at a time to examine every detail of the furniture. Grim told him to sit down, and he chose the rug in the center of the floor, gathering his brown cloak about him and arranging its folds as if to protect himself from unseen evil.

"How did you get as far as this without surrendering your rifle?" Grim asked him.

"By damn, Jimgrim, it was either that or not at all. If I had come by way of El-Kerak and taken the bridge over the Jordan the Sikhs on watch there would have been too many for me. They would have required it according to custom."

"They would have given you a receipt," said Grim. "You could have had it back on your return."

"Maybe. A rifle is a man's life. Who leaves his life in a stranger's keeping, against words on a scrap of paper in a foreign speech? I came by the south end of the Dead Sea, avoiding Sikhs and such folk. At El-Kalil there was an officer — an Englishman — a young cock-sparrow full of mirth and brains, who bade me give my rifle up. But I gave him talk instead of it. 'In the name of Allah the Omnipotent,' said I, 'you shall fight me for the rifle if you want it. I killed a German for it in the war; now it is mine until another man kills me. Maybe thou art the man,' said I, 'although I think not.' "

"That would be Captain de Crespigny, I dare say?" Grim suggested, smiling.

"Aye, that was the youngster's name. A straight-standing child with a smooth face. *Mashallah!* He told me he is Governor of El-Kalil! Did he lie?"

"Not he. What did he answer you about the rifle?"

"He laughed, and said it would be a shame to kill such a specimen as me. Whereat I started on my way again, but he called me back and wrote out a permission, lest, as he said, I should slay all the soldiers in Jerusalem."

"Did you show the permit to the police here?" Grim asked him.

"By damn, not I! I let the dogs bay after me! What I have in my pouch is my affair. Who has permission from the Governor of El-Kalil needs no favors from lesser folk; and besides, he might not have been the governor after all. Who am I to stop and trade curses with policemen?"

"Let's see what de Crespigny wrote," said Grim.

The Bedouin reached into the mysterious recesses of an under-garment and produced a greasy, thumb-marked sheet torn from a memorandum book. It was folded criss-cross fashion, and addressed in pencil to Grim. Grim read it, smiled, and passed it on to me. It ran:

> *Dear Grim, this fellow Aroun, of the Saoud clan swears he is a friend of yours. I rather hope it's true. I like him. But if he's a liar, send him back this way, and I'll have some fun with him in the jail here.*
> *Yours,*
> *C. de Crespigny.*

Grim handed the note back to its bearer, who pouched it proudly. It has probably done yeoman service since in the heart of

Arabia, displayed to folk who can't read as proof conclusive of any wild statement its owner cares to make.

"Well, what message do you bring?" Grim asked him.

"Hassan ben Saoud says you are to come to him."

"To what place? When?"

"Now, at once, to Abu Kem, which is two days' camel-ride to the south and east of Abu Lissan. He said, 'Tell Jimgrim to do no dallying but come at once.' "

Grim crossed one leg over the other and leaned back in his armchair lazily.

"In a hurry, is he? What's the trouble?"

"He said: 'No need to tell the nature of the trouble. Let it be enough that there *is* trouble. Jimgrim interfered between me and Ali Higg of Petra. By a trick he came between me and sure victory. I had pledged my word, and I kept my word. Now Jimgrim keep his word to me. He promised to come and help me at my call. It should therefore be enough to say that Hassan ben Saoud the Avenger summons him. If he doesn't answer that, let him go the way of all dogs and I will do without him. But I think he is not a dog, and will answer the summons.' So spake Saoud the Avenger and I rode a seven days' journey to repeat his words."

"Don't you know what the difficulty is?" asked Grim.

"Wallahi! That I do!"

"Is it a secret?"

"As secret as the devil's hiding-place! Some say that King Solomon has come back to Earth and has the witches working for him. Others say that the devil in person has made his abode in Arabia. There has been a comet, and the great well at Abu Kem has run dry."

"I can't catch comets in a net, or fix dry wells," said Grim. "Witches are none of my business either. I wouldn't know how to deal with the devil, and as for King Solomon, I guess as much of him as isn't dead is hard to find. You'll have to tell me a plainer tale, than that, my friend."

"But ben Saoud the Avenger has your promise. What is the word of Jimgrim worth, then?"

"I didn't promise ben Saoud to do exactly what he said at any time. He demanded that, and I refused. What I did promise was to help him in my own way, if he should get into difficulty. You've got to tell me what the difficulty is."

"By Allah, not so! When I call my camel he must come."

"I am no man's camel," answered Grim.

"If a man owes me money and I demand it, he must pay. I am not required to tell him what I need the money for."

"Does ben Saoud realize what it means for me to get men together and make that journey? Is he so hard pressed that he feels entitled to put me to all that expense and inconvenience?"

"By Allah, Jimgrim, you know me," our visitor answered. "You know I am the Avenger's trusted man. You hear my words. You hear me say I speak for the Avenger. You hear me say he needs you. You made the Avenger a promise. Keep it!"

"I intend to," Grim answered.

"*Taib.*"

"But answer this: Which would likely be of most use, a friend with his eyes shut, or a friend who can see all sides of a matter and so make preparation in advance?"

"A friend is a friend, Jimgrim."

"True; and a rifle is a rifle, but some shoot straight and others don't. Suppose the rifle is supplied with cartridges that don't fit?"

"Well; this is a matter of life and death. Come well armed and supplied. Bring machine guns and six regiments if you have them," said our visitor.

Grim laughed aloud at that, and clapped his hands for the servant to bring coffee.

"You fellows believe in just one solution for all problems, don't you!" he said.

"True, Jimgrim. It is the law of Allah that death solves everything. A man is righteous; he dies, and enters paradise; shall he complain? A man does evil; he is slain and hurled into Jehannum; the survivors have his goods, and Allah smiles. Without death in the reckoning all would be talk and no solution. A good rifle and a sharp sword are Allah's arbiters."

The coffee came, and we drank it in comparative silence. The snorts and lip-smacking of our visitor were intended for a compliment — an echo, as it were, of inward ecstacy, not to be confounded with mere noise.

"Are you fit to travel?" Grim asked at last.

"*Inshallah,* I would like to go tonight, but my camel is exhausted."

"I can lend you another camel. We'll give your beast a day's rest, and I'll bring it along after you. You'll start back at moonrise?"

"By your honor's favor."

"Then tell ben Saoud the Avenger this: I'm coming at once,

because of the promise. If he needs help badly, I'll do my best."

"God give your honor long life!"

"But it is neither simple nor convenient just now for me to come. If I find that the Avenger has sent for me without good reason, not only will my promise be wiped out, but the balance will swing heavily the other way. Will you tell him that?"

"If I live."

"I shall start tomorrow night. If on second thought the Avenger decides he can do without me, let him send back a messenger to meet me on the road. In that case, well and good; I will turn aside to important business, and no harm will have been done. But unless such a messenger meets me, I will go forward, and the Avenger will have hard work to make his peace with me afterwards, if this should prove to be false alarm."

"Better write all that in a letter, Jimgrim."

"Why? The Avenger sent his message by word of mouth to me."

"But if I should die on the road, or be made prisoner?"

"In that case a letter would certainly fall into wrong hands. No. If there is to be any writing, the Avenger shall do it over his seal and signature at my dictation."

"By Allah and His Prophet, these are words at random anyhow!" said our visitor. "The affair is serious, as you shall see. The Avenger believes you are the only man capable of understanding, to say nothing of solving it. He holds you to your promise, but he is no ingrate. Show him the way out of this, and you may name your own terms afterwards."

"Trust me. I will!" Grim answered dourly.

"He who keeps promises shall find that promises are kept," said the Bedouin sententiously.

SO, BY A BOLT from the blue, as it were, our activities were outlined for the next three weeks. All Grim's immediate plans were swept into the discard, and we began there and then the always exhilarating business of preparing for a fresh campaign. There isn't any greater fun on earth than that, whatever the subsequent outcome. I believe that wars are made more often than not by the fun men have in getting ready for them; and the misery of the last is straightway forgotten in the sport of preparation for the next.

Lord knows, I've had as much trouble in wild lands as most men of my age, but I'm as thrilled as the greenest tenderfoot at the sight of blankets being rolled; tents made ready; and, above all, saddles. Saddles and sails — the day has not yet come when gasolene or steam can quite replace them; they are rather more than symbols in the desert of this latter-day efficiency, and their lure has the old heart-tug in it. And camel-saddles are the best of all.

Nevertheless, the trappings are as nothing compared to the men who shall use them. Given good men, you can campaign on a shoe-string, and the worst of starting in a hurry is the risk of taking with you handsome fellows who will lie down in a pinch, and quarrel over trifles twenty leagues from home.

That was where Grim enjoyed his great advantage. He was under no necessity to employ the alleged efficient hirelings, who make nightmares of most journeys in that country. The absurd delusion that a jail-sentence unfits a man for official jobs obsesses governments, so the men who ought to be in jail get government employment and the fellows who have learned by sharp experience that off-side isn't in the game are left off-side without a chance to put their schooling to fair use.

But, being on short allowance for expenses, Grim was not only permitted, but encouraged to pick his men from among the reputed undesirables. The widows of the riffraff don't draw pensions, and there aren't any union rates of pay; but the riffraff, if you want to call them that, are usually grateful for small mercies.

The same rule applies, with obvious exceptions, to enlisted men. It isn't always wise to choose the men who know the inside of the regimental clink, but some men with scandalous defaulter sheets are rebels against monotony rather than against discipline, and what such fellows hunger for is interesting work.

The first man Grim sent for was Narayan Singh, our Sikh friend, who had been with us on one or two adventures — the best man in his regiment by almost any way of reckoning but, as it happened, in disgrace — and in the cells — just then.

There wasn't anything they could have done but put him in the cells. The cantonment life had bored him badly after our last trip, and the hooch they sell in the out-of-bounds slums of Palestine works miracles with the sign reversed. As a rule when he is drunk he likes to parade without his pants, but on this occasion he had turned up stark naked on the drill-ground and, being a man of muscle and adroitness, had provided ten men and a sergeant with an hour's strenuous work catching him and putting him in irons.

Good soldiers, like good workmen at any trade, possess friends in high places and corresponding advantages unguessed by the ranks of mere malingerers. A telephone message to Narayan Singh's colonel relieved more individuals than one; you could almost feel over the wire the satisfaction with which Goodenough agreed to continue the Sikh's "punishment" — to make a horrible example of him, in fact — by ordering him out of cells at once and away on special service under Grim.

I am told that not a man in the regiment smiled next morning when the order was made known. There are people — Sikhs among them — who can enjoy a joke without disturbing the conventions.

Narayan Singh arrived that evening, resplendent in a brand-new khaki uniform for which his pay would probably be docked for months to come. His beard was oiled and curled; his dark eyes had already lost the dissipated glare that goes with drunkenness; and somewhere in the middle of the black hair was a streak of flashing white teeth that showed first as he loomed enormous in the doorway of our sitting-room with the night behind him.

Not a word of explanation or excuses. Grim and he understood each other. Narayan Singh saluted, Grim nodded, and there all ceremony ceased.

"We're going back of Abu Lissan, Narayan Singh."

"Wherever you say, *sahib*."

"It's a blind affair. No knowing what's in the wind."

"So long as the affair is blind, and not we, let the wind blow how it will, *bahadur*. Who else goes?"

"We'll take the old gang."

"Better so. Old dogs hunt best."

"Suppose you get away to El-Kalil tonight. Take a Ford car, and have the driver hurry. Call at the governorate first; then roust out Ali Baba in the *suk* [bazaar] and tell him to get ready to start tomorrow with his sixteen sons. If any of the sons are away, or can't be spared, or happen to be in jail on serious charges, tell Ali Baba to find substitutes. But if any of them are in jail for a minor offense, ask Captain de Crespigny to release them. You can't travel as a Sikh beyond El-Kalil; dress as a Pathan; here's money; account to me for it. That's all, I think."

There was something else, though. Narayan Singh stood without speaking, motionless, like a great meek simpleton — he who is neither meek nor simple in any circumstance. He was technically still a prisoner, and his rifle and bayonet were locked away until such time as Grim should report his sentence served. It was beneath his dignity to refer to the matter, yet a dog without teeth would be happier than that Sikh without weapons.

It was about a minute before Grim understood the situation. "Hadn't you better go for that car?" he said.

But Narayan Singh continued to stand in silence.

"You don't need a note from me. The driver knows you. Just jump in the car and tell him where to go."

But the Sikh's expression remained wooden, and Grim looked puzzled. The world was more likely to come to an end from surfeit of morals than that Narayan Singh would balk at active service and responsibility. But an almost unnoticeable gesture of helplessness — a relaxing of the muscles of arms and shoulders — provided the clue, and Grim sat down at his desk to write a note to the Governor of El-Kalil.

"Give that to Captain de Crespigny, and he'll let you pick over the governorate armory. I don't suppose what he's got there is any good, but you'll have to manage."

The Sikh grinned contentedly, saluted, and was gone. Until midnight we two overhauled old maps, Grim's old notebooks, pistols, kit, and what not; and we were about to turn in when the same Ford car that had taken Narayan Singh came to a clattering, tooting halt outside the gate, and some one began pounding on the front door.

WE WERE USED TO midnight messengers, for Grim's business works day and night. It was likely enough some scaremonger who had begged a ride on the strength of wild tales of a rising somewhere. Grim went to the door with his face set ready to cut short the interview, but a moment later ushered into the sitting room no less a personage than Ali Baba, father and grandfather of the sixteen thieves of El-Kalil.

Now what is it that makes a nod of confidential recognition from such a man seem more like balm of Gilead than the smile of a proconsul? Ali Baba was a thief, and the proud progenitor of thieves. I don't suppose there is a species of raw rascality that he and his have not been intimately connected with at some stage of their careers; and the last time I had anything to do with the old villain he stole my good repeating pistol, and made a song about it, which he and his sons sang repeatedly thereafter in my presence, it being part of their creed that no theft is really profitable. or amusing unless the victim knows who perpetrated it.

I should say you couldn't find a more disreputable character than Ali Baba in the whole of the Near East — and mind you, that is a broad statement — yet the old man's nod to me was like the handshake of a friend.

Well, I didn't make the world. I'm telling facts, not trying to explain things.

Ali Baba was perturbed. His gray beard bristled with excitement, and his dark eyes shone with nervousness. As he sat down cross-legged on the couch his wrinkled hands twitched; and though he normally looks bland and respectable enough to be custodian of a saint's tomb, there was an air about him now of impotent rascality caught napping. He wasn't exactly in a rage, but he was ready to blow up at the first excuse, and his right and left hand went in turns to the dagger stuck in his waist-cloth.

But after he had sat down he went through all the long formality of Arab greeting, first to Grim, and then all over again to me — question and reply — question and reply — all about our health, the state of our bowels, glory be to Allah the condition of his own inside — the weather — the crops — the price of camel-feed — then, suddenly:

"That Sikh Narayan Singh came, Jimgrim. He bade me be ready tomorrow with my sons and God knows how many camels for an expedition to last a month."

Grim nodded, smiling. He smiles with his eyes at Arabs in a way that seems to break down all suspicion and open the way for confidences.

"But it is impossible. By Allah, it can't be done."

"You've been doing things that can't be done all your life," Grim answered. "What's the trouble, O father of impossibilities?"

"I have a business in. hand. It is profitable. All my sons and grandsons are engaged in it. Every camel I own, and twenty more that I have hired are in training for a long trip. The loads are made up. All is ready. We would have been gone day before yesterday, *inshallah,* if that young dog they have made Governor of El-Kalil hadn't got wind of it and set his cursed police to prevent us. He threatens the lot of us with jail if we as much as move. May Allah change his face! He only let me out of El-Kalil tonight to see you, Jimgrim, on condition that the driver promised not to set me down anywhere between there and here."

"Uh-huh. Young de Crespigny has wisdom."

"Wisdom, has he! *Taib.* I have business! Listen, Jimgrim; I have been a friend of yours. You and I have seen the color of the face of death together. When have I refused to do you a service?

I have risked my neck, and the necks of all my sons for your sake —"

"Wasn't it worth while?"

"Yes, by Allah! But it is your turn to do me a favor. You have power in the land. When you suggest, the Administration listens. When you request, what you ask is granted. So say the word, and let me go about this business."

"What is the nature of the business?" Grim inquired cautiously. But subsequent events convinced me that he knew very well what the business was, only it is part of his method almost never to admit how much he knows.

"We had a prosperous thieving business, you know, Jimgrim, until you came to El-Kalil and put an end to it. There are no cleverer thieves than we, but you are a devil, and we can't outwit you."

"Well?"

"A man and his sons must live."

"That seems to be an axiom."

"But only a Jew can live legally in this land, nowadays. We are not used to these new laws and restrictions, and can't understand them, because they are not in the Koran and we had no hand in making them. Under the Turks there was law, but that was good. All men understood it. There was a law against this, and a law against that — there were laws against all that was desirable; but there was a price for breaking the law which could be arranged beforehand with the Turk; the price varied, but a good bargainer could make a profit.

"But these young British idiots won't play that game. The Turkish governor used to make his own laws, which everybody understood; but these British infants, such as de Crespigny, enforce laws made elsewhere by other people, which neither they nor any other man except a Jew can possibly understand, and though you can bribe a policeman to his heart's content, the man whose orders he must obey is incorruptible."

"Too bad," Grim commented, when the old man paused for breath.

"So it became necessary to arrange for business beyond the border, where there are no British to enforce whatever the Jews require. And when I took my sons on that last trip with you to Petra, we all kept our ears to the ground."

Ali Baba paused again, this time in order to judge how much it might be safe to tell. His foxy old eyes blinked keenly for several seconds, trying to read faces in the jumpy light of the reading lamp: but there was only a smile hovering about Grim's eyes, and as I knew nothing it was easy for me to look the part of a stuffed owl. Grim raised his eyebrows at last, and relighted his pipe, to get the old man to talking again.

"So it happened that Mujrim, my oldest-born, went on a little expedition all alone. There was great risk, but he is a great adventurer, and he was in Allah's keeping; so he came back —"

"With a bag of gold-dust, which he sold for cash to Aaron Cohen," said Grim. "We all know that. Go on."

"You all know it, you say? Who are all of you that know it? *Bismillah!* Is there no such thing as a secret any more? Cohen swore he would not tell. Curse him, he shall eat his oath whole, and feel the knife that carves it inside his belly!"

"Cohen didn't tell," said Grim.

"Then, if you are not the devil, Jimgrim, he is your father and patron saint! How did you find out?"

"Easily. Cohen resold the gold-dust to the bank. The bank was obliged to report the purchase. It was known that Cohen had been to El-Kalil, and took a lot of cash with him; and there hasn't been gold-dust in El-Kalil for generations. He returned without the cash, but with the gold-dust. It was known that your son Mujrim had been away, and in which direction. There has been gold in Arabia ever since Solomon's time. Two and two make four. Go on, tell me the rest of it."

"*Mashallah!* To tell you things is like repeating the day's lesson to a *m'allim!* Tell me how much you know, Jimgrim, and I will answer whether it's true or false."

"Uh-uh! You came here to ask me a favor. State your case, O father of evasion."

"Well; that gold-dust was given as a trust to Mujrim. We are known far and wide as honorable thieves. A man can have confidence in our promises."

"Which man in this instance?"

"Jmil Ras."

Grim nodded. "Is he as handsome as his name implies?"

"I haven't seen him, Jimgrim. Mujrim tells me he is a wonder to behold. Surely he pays handsomely, and knows a trustworthy fellow when he sees him. After deducting a percentage for profit and expenses — half and half was the condition named, but the Jew cheated us about the price of gold-dust and it would not have been fair to charge the loss against our portion — the remainder was to be spent for certain goods, which we were to deliver by camel to a place beyond Abu Lissan.

"Now we have kept faith; we have laid out his share of the money with great care having sent even as far as Egypt for some of the things; and because Jmil Ras's share of the money was not sufficient, we invested some of ours, trusting to his fairness to make it good with interest. We are ready to do our part in full, Jimgrim, but a puppy of a governor prevents — may Allah cause his bowels to burn seven days and seven nights a week! Unless you help us, Jimgrim, we must fail; and who then can repay that money to Jmil Ras?"

"And if I help you?"

"Name your own terms, Jimgrim! Speak, and I agree!"

"All right. You may make the trip, but I'm coming with you."

"*Il hamdulillah!* May Allah bless your sons and grandsons and give you old age to enjoy them, Jimgrim! I swore no friend of yours could appeal to you in vain!"

"But as you suggested, it is I who name the terms," Grim continued, and Ali Baba peered at him once more like a fox.

"Whatever is possible, Jimgrim. Whatever is possible. There were things that even the Prophet could not do."

"You supply me and my friends with camels and escort as far as I choose to go. You and your sons obey me first, last, and all the time. My business comes first, but I pay no wages, and nothing for camel-hire. On those conditions, I will help you to deliver the goods to Jmil Ras, and we start tomorrow night. Do you agree?"

"In the name of Him who never sleeps, it is a bargain, Jimgrim! Allah makes all things easy!"

Chapter V

"Suppose we stage an accident!"

"THERE ARE A THOUSAND ways to anywhere, but only one will serve," says the Arab proverb; so we took our former road by way of El-Kalil, although the simplest course would have been to let Ali Baba and his men come to us and then ride straight eastward from Jerusalem, crossing the Jordan by the iron bridge. We might have saved a day's march that way, but should undoubtedly have loosed a thousand tongues.

Ali Baba, like many another old man, needed little sleep and preferred that little in the afternoon; so back he went that night to El-Kalil to muster his sons and make all ready. He had told us the camels were in training, which means they had been kept without water for constantly increasing periods; they had now gone five days without a drink, and his most important business was to water them at dawn, superintending with experienced eye to make sure that each beast took its fill; for they will fool you if not watched, and lie down to die of drought the third day out from home.

We silenced the tongues of Jerusalem by changing into disguise next morning before we started. It's easy for Grim, who simply changes clothes and is an Arab; but to fix me up as an Indian, which is my only chance of being mistaken for a Moslem, takes time and trouble.

My head had to be shaved, for one thing; fortunately for the purpose I have a dark beard, which grows fast, and by removing all hair from where a white man grows it and allowing it to bristle and curl on my jaws instead, I can pass muster as a rather respectable-looking Indian *darwaish* — which is a fanatical person with a taint of learning, who wanders at the prick of religious fanaticism.

Being a big man, I naturally look enormous in the narrow-legged cotton pantaloons and straight smock under a sort of frock-coat thing that well-to-do Indians affect. But that doesn't matter if I pose as from Lahore, where the giants of the North have left their physical stamp on more than one conquered race. The shaved head offsets the normal Arab contempt for Indians by creating the suggestion of religious authority, and a necklace of prayer-beads does the rest. The costume is comfortable enough, but when you put one of those great brown Bedouin cloaks on top of it, you're likely to sweat the fat off before riding many miles.

Grim and I rode horseback as far as Hebron, cantering the first few miles because of the risk of my being recognized until the dark whiskers should conceal a jawbone such as — so Grim tells me — might have been used by Samson when he slew the thousand Philistines.

If a thing is made known in Jerusalem it is multiplied a thousand-fold in Baghdad ten days afterward; Damascus passes it on by way of Beirut to the Golden Horn, and in about a month there is a question asked about it by a labor member in the House of Commons.

A little later, New York prints a paragraph about it in between the murders and divorces, and some one on the Stock Exchange sells the whole list short and starts rumors of war. It isn't a bad plan to avoid observation when you're off on secret business.

But there were few folk abroad that morning, except peasants, mostly women and asses laden with stuff for market with a leisurely, lordly man or two consuming cigarets in charge. They gave us a wide berth to avoid our dust, and also because we had rifles, which might have meant we were policemen. There are other places in the world where the police take toll of passers-by, but none where it is done more thoroughly, because the evil of the Turks lives after them.

An hour after daybreak the land lay white as a bone and the color of amethyst in the baking sun. The glimpse we had of the Dead Sea was of a sparkling sapphire set in the rust and sulfur of the Moab hills; and Jerusalem behind us was a gray-white sepulchre. There wasn't any milk and honey overflowing, nor any balm in the wind that brought dust devils courtesying and waltzing all the way from Egypt.

We were two dry men who drew rein at the governorate, reverently grateful for the luke-warm drinks mixed by de Crespigny, who prides himself with all the man-of-the-worldishness of six-and-twenty years on some attainments he does not possess. You can forgive him false pride in weird formulas for spoiling liquor, because he does not know that he is a genius at keeping peace among ungovernable men, and speaks of the impossible that happens regularly in his "parish," as he calls it, as "just my luck. I was born under a lucky star."

We were all day long in El-Kalil, talking things over with de Crespigny and dozing through the afternoon. There was information shared by Grim and de Crespigny that they did not trouble to explain to me, although they discussed it in my presence and did not try particularly hard to keep it secret from me. It seemed they both knew this man Jmil Ras, to whom Ali Baba proposed to deliver merchandise, and it was the nature of the merchandise that gave them most concern. Incidentally, it made me prick my ears more than if the camel-loads had contained machine guns and ammunition.

"Spades," said de Crespigny, "shovels, sieves, sledge-hammers, crowbars, picks, bags of cement — that all might be for building a fort or something; but here's the unexplainable — nine lengths of steel rail stolen from the railway stores at Ludd, three big sheaf-blocks pinched from a Greek boat laid up at Jaffa for repairs, and three great lumps of hard steel weighing more than a hundred pounds apiece, one with a hole through the narrow end, one shaped something like a bottle with a big nob where the cork would be, and the third an old-fashioned scale-weight by the look of it, with a bar shaped in the top to lift it by."

"Do you suppose the shapes are design or haphazard?" asked Grim.

"Both, I should say. There were plenty to choose from; they were being used as ballast by a coast-wise trading felucca, and Ali Baba offered such a price for his pick that the little captain saw the superior virtues of sacks filled with pebbles from the beach, and traded. I imagine Ali Baba chose the shapes that came nearest to specifications; but what d'you suppose Jmil Ras wants with them?"

"Well," said Grim, "he paid for them with gold-dust, didn't he? How would you go about getting gold out of quartz?" he asked, turning suddenly to me.

"Dolly it out with weights dropped by hand from a pulley," I answered. "I've worked out enough to pay for proper machinery in that way more than once; but it's hopeless unless the stuff assays a good many ounces to the ton, because you can't recover half of it. He'll need mercury —"

"Ali Baba has been moving heaven and earth for mercury and cyanide. Not a chance of getting either, though," said de Crespigny.

"I know where there's cyanide," Grim answered, "but mercury is another matter."

"Who is Jmil Ras anyhow?" I asked, breaking my rule of not asking questions. But I might as well have broken a plate or something of that sort. De Crespigny glanced swiftly at Grim, who is much more expert at concealing the fact that he knows and prefers not to tell. Grim's face didn't change a particle as he answered me.

"We aim to discover that on this trip. Where in thunder can we get cyanide?"

I made a suggestion at random.

"Unless the Huns left some behind on their retreat —" And suddenly Grim remembered. "Weren't they experimenting with the glass business here, Crep? Took over a building in the glass-makers' quarter, didn't they? Put in a new-fangled furnace with a fuel-saving contraption to regulate the heat? Anybody been in there for a year?"

"No. Enemy property. Place is sealed up."

"If I remember rightly there was a big steel ball full of mercury that opened and closed the draft in some mysterious way," said Grim.

"Yes, maybe; but we can't break that seal," de Crespigny objected.

"I wonder how much mercury was in the thing, and whether it's there now. How much would we need?" asked Grim.

"Not much," said I. "An ounce or two would be better than none. You can use the stuff over and over. Depends on the scale of operations."

One piece of information Grim could not keep to himself. He was excited. The poker player's mask that he assumes when on a hot scent was growing uncommonly transparent; his left fist was clenched tight, and his forehead wrinkled into whorls.

"We've got to get that mercury or cyanide, Crep."

De Crespigny laughed and shook his head.

"Can't be done, old dear. Steal anything you want except enemy property. Can't have the Crown Prince tossing us *tu quoque.* I'll accept your receipt for anything you fancy, bones of Abraham included, but no Hun stuff — unless, of course, you care to override my authority."

"Wouldn't consider doing that, of course, but see here, Crep," said Grim with more impassioned earnestness in his voice than I had ever heard him use. "We've got to find a way of contriving this. It's Feisul's chance! The French are going to chase Feisul out of Damascus; that's a foregone conclusion, and about the best thing that can happen to him, for he hasn't a chance to make good as king of united Syria.

"He'll go to Europe, where he'll beard the politicians in their den and remind them of the promises they made when they wanted him in the war on any terms. They can't deny that they made the promises; and not even that gang could deny that Feisul and his Arabs made it possible to win the war. They promised him an independent Arab kingdom, and they'll have to make good. If anything on earth is certain, it's a dead sure bet that they'll send Feisul back to carve out an Arab government across the Jordan. He'll probably get Baghdad too to begin with."

"Let's hope so anyhow," laughed de Crespigny, "but what has that got to do with quicksilver? I'm acting deputy custodian of enemy property just now, and though I get no extra pay for it, a job's a job."

"It's this way," Grim answered. "What Feisul is going to need most of all is money. If he has to depend on European high finance he's likely to get ditched again before he has half a chance to make good. But if we can fix him up with an independent gold-mine, situated in Arabia beyond the zone of mandates and the reach of company promoters, rich enough in ore to pay for machinery out of profits, Feisul is a made man. D'you get me?"

"Yes, but that don't get you the quicksilver! Besides, it seems to be Jmil Ras's gold. What has Feisul got to do with it?"

"Leave that to me. Jmil Ras wouldn't send for mercury unless he needed it the worst way. Mercury and cyanide — good Lord! He must have known that inquiries for stuff like that would set the Intelligence Department by the ears. What worries me is that the next thing you know, the Zionists will hear of it."

"What if they do?"

"They need money."

"All right. They've no claim to Arabia?"

"They'd no claim to Palestine that anyone out here could see; but here they are. If they claim Palestine because King Solomon built a temple in Jerusalem, what's to stop them from claiming the quartz out of which Solomon roasted his gold? This is a case for head-work. If we don't supply Jmil Ras with what he wants, sooner or later he's going to sell his prospect in the open market. We've got to help him make a killing, and then bottle up the secret until Feisul's time comes. Don't you see, Crep?"

"Sounds all right, if you can satisfy Jmil Ras. But I won't break that enemy property seal for Feisul or anyone — not even for you, James Schuyler Grim; and I count you my friend at that."

"Never mind me. Think of Feisul."

"He's a friend, too, but I'm custodian."

"Suppose we stage an accident. How thick is the door? The windows are iron-barred, I remember, but a camel might kick the door in."

I had never seen Grim so desperate for an expedient. He is usually reserved to the point of taciturnity, and stolidly averse to argument, especially when he has a plan in mind. But now there were actually great beads of sweat standing on his forehead, and his normally quiet face had the keen expression of a heavy plunger watching a horse-race.

"Not if I can keep away the camel," laughed de Crespigny. "No, Grim. You've either got to override me on the score of seniority — in which case I shall have to phone Jerusalem, of course — or the seal stays where it is."

"Well, I guess you're right, Crep. Damn it to Hell!"

Grim looked sharply at me, and just at that moment Narayan Singh came and stood in the doorway to ask for orders. He was dressed in his usual disguise as a Pathan, and what with the rifle and two bandoliers that he had picked out from the governorate armory he looked sufficiently humorously savage even for that part. Like me, he looks enormous in clothes of that kind. It occurred to me to wonder which of us two was the heaviest, and that — added to Grim's swift glance — gave me another thought.

"I'll speak to Narayan Singh," said I, and left the room.

"In the name of all wonders, *sahib,* what has happened to our Jimgrim, *sahib,*?" the Sikh asked me when we reached the street.

"Do you know any of our Western mythology?" I asked him. "Who were the ancient gods, for instance?"

"They made me read that nonsense in the school where I learned English."

"You remember then that Mercury was the messenger of the gods?"

"Aye, wings on his ankles he had."

"There's reason to believe the gentleman is hiding in a German glass-factory in El-Kalil; but like the spirit in the vase in the Arab fish-story, he's sealed up. Nobody's allowed to break the seal. But if you and I can get him out and leave the seal unbroken, I know how to make him coax gold out of rock, and Jimgrim thinks he can make him set a new king on an ancient throne."

"Well and good. We be two resourceful men. Lead the way and let us try."

"I don't know the way," I answered, "but Ali Baba does, and he has sixteen thieves to lend a hand."

So we threaded the mazy *suk* of El-Kalil and found old Ali Baba in the camel-*khan* sitting in the shade on top of a pile of roped loads, smoking his water-pipe and lecturing his sons. When I told him what I had in mind it did not take him ten seconds to decide to show the way.

But we did not go trooping through the narrow streets to call attention to ourselves; nineteen men, seventeen of whom were notorious thieves, all headed in the same direction, would have given El-Kalil a theme to talk about for weeks. Ali Baba knew a way over the roofs that was hot, devious, and risky, because the harem folk don't encourage that kind of liberty; but we ran less risk of observation that way, for the heat had driven every one indoors, or into the shadow of the ancient arches.

IN LESS THAN TEN minutes all nineteen of us were standing on a flat roof with a high stone chimney at one end, which Ali Baba guaranteed to be the sealed-up German factory. I got down to the street and made sure, for there was no sense in burgling the wrong place. The seal was on the door all right, and the door was of solid olive-wood, which no camel in the universe could have kicked down, although any of the long-necked beasts can kick from either end about as hard as three mules. The windows were all barred with thick iron. I couldn't find another door, and there were no weak places in the walls; so I climbed up to the roof again. The roofs of El-Kalil are of stone, at least a foot thick and cemented; there was no chance of breaking through without making noise enough to disturb the whole city's siesta. I had hoped to find a trap-door, which Narayan Singh's weight and mine combined might break.

I don't like lying as a general thing, but taking one consideration with another and the fact that we were burgling Hun property, I wouldn't have minded swearing that was an accident. However, there was no trap-door, so I was saved from perjury.

The chimney was the only thing for it, and the top of that was barred across with an iron grille; but the job had been done hastily and the ends of the iron weren't set deep in the masonry. Mujrim, Ali Baba's oldest and biggest son, fetched a long piece of wood, and the grille came loose in about two minutes when we used that as a lever and he, the Sikh, and I exerted our combined strength.

Those expert thieves would have gone down the chimney like rats into a hole, but as I would have to show them which was the mercury and how to get it, I decided to go first; and not being an old-timer at their trade, they had to lower me. So they made a long rope of their waist-cloths, making one end fast under my arms, and I went down feet first — slowly, because the big knots in the rope didn't render freely over the chimney coping, which was about a foot higher than the head of a man standing on the roof. In fact, you had to stand on a man's shoulders in order to get into the chimney to begin with.

It was an idiotic thing to go first. We should have sent the smallest man to prospect for us. I am bigger than Narayan Singh, and even than Mujrim, and although what isn't bone in my great bulk is mostly muscle, sheer strength doesn't fit a man, any more than wealth is said to, for passing through the needle's eye.

In addition to getting stuffier and rougher as I went down, the chimney narrowed, for some ultra-scientific reason known best to the Germans who designed it, and I stuck twice and nearly suffocated before reaching a queerly shaped black hole at the bottom, lined with soot. By that time I had lost a lot of skin off my knees and elbows and was about two-thirds choked in the bargain. Hardly any light came down the chimney, of course, but by groping I discovered that the only opening into the factory was a slot about six inches deep and two feet wide on about a level with my waist as I stood on a deep cushion of soot.

I hated to be hauled up again. It was going to hurt for one thing, and for another such soot as I hadn't scraped off on the way down was going to fall on my head. However, there seemed nothing else for it, so I shook the rope to call their attention above, and the whole thing fell down on top of me. A moment later the square of blue sky overhead was shut off by Narayan Singh's head and shoulders, leaning over to inquire if I was all right. I wouldn't be surprised to hear that I used bad language. However, that wasn't the end of the world, of course. They could get another rope and lower it, and no doubt there was air enough down there to keep a man alive indefinitely, although it did not feel like it; my lungs, in fact, felt full of soot already, and the sensation was of having been buried alive.

Narayan Singh kept asking idiotic questions, and one way and another my temper got the better of me. I could have thrashed the fools who dropped that rope, and killed the men who designed such a trap of a chimney. I shouted to Narayan Singh to take his wooden head out of the light, and in a huge rage at the notion of having to be hauled up empty-handed, grimy as a sweep, to be laughed at by those Arabs, I began to grope about with my fingers in the dark.

The hole I stood in was so small that I could run my hands over every inch of the walls without shifting my feet, and I scraped the soot off, thinking that perhaps the miscreants who built it might have left a man-hole somewhere.

But all I discovered was a round iron plate that covered a hole about large enough to admit a man's arm. It was fixed in place as firmly as a strong-room door, being bolted apparently to another plate on the outside. My wrath boiled over entirely at that discovery. You know how unreasonable a man can be in a tight place, when he feels he has brought his trouble on himself and would rather pass the blame along? I don't get that way often, but when I do I see fire.

I wanted to do damage — began to grope with my fingers for something I could seize on and break; and I found a crack in the masonry extending from the bottom of that iron plate all the way down in a zigzag to the level of my feet, where the piled-up soot had filled and covered it.

It wasn't reason, but downright savagery that made me set my shoulder against that crack, brace both feet against the opposite wall, and exert every ounce of strength I had in me. I thought of Samson among the Philistines breaking down the galleries on his tormentors; of Horatius holding the bridge over the Tiber in ancient Rome — Oh, of loads of splendid things that had no conceivable bearing on my predicament; and with the fury of the Berserker that lives somewhere underneath my normal calm I shoved until my muscles swelled and cracked and crimson fire blazed under my shut eyelids.

Something had to give, or I should have been lamed for life by my own exertion. I came within an ace of serious injury as it was; for suddenly the whole wall of the chimney below that iron plate and to one side of the crack gave outward, and I shot my full length on to a smooth stone floor all mixed up with the falling masonry. And there I lay for I dare say sixty seconds, wondering whether I were dead, and if not, why?

Narayan Singh's excited booming down the chimney made me begin to think again like a more or less rational being. Alive or dead, there will always be something to do I reckon. I wasn't bruised worth mentioning, but I had made a hole in that chimney wall that you could have wheeled a barrow into, so either the manufacturers' tables of the tensile strength of cement are away off the mark, or else that was local stuff put up without analysis or guarantee. I yelled up the chimney to the gang to get another rope, and set about exploring.

There was the new-fangled furnace sure enough, and it did not seem to have been used much. In front of it, protruding from a neck-like tube was the steel ball Grim had spoken of — not much bigger than a good-sized coconut, which it furthermore resembled, in that its only opening connected with the stem, or neck. There was a sledge-hammer near by, and I might possibly have broken the ball off; but it occurred to me that people with enough ambition to import that furnace would be likely to provide for accidents. So I looked further, kicking open a locked door in a partition wall.

The first glimpse inside set me to whistling so loud that Narayan Singh bellowed down the chimney again to ask what I wanted. A long table set against the wall of a narrow, room was piled with experimental pieces of rolled glass, and the back of nearly every perfect piece was silvered! Who couldn't love a German after that? I changed my mind about the Huns, forgave them for the chimney, and began to look about for the store of quicksilver, nervously refusing attention to a persistent fear that some manager with time on his hands might have used up all the furnace's reserve supply in the course of a private experiment.

It turned out that he had done just that. A small container that had held the stuff was empty in a corner on the floor; but that wasn't all. On another bench was more rolled glass all laid out ready to be silvered, as if the experiments had gone far enough and mirror-making was about to begin on a small commercial scale.

Now the man who had made those preparations might have been waiting for the quicksilver to be imported; but in that case it was hardly likely that he would have laid the glass ready in rows. So

I kicked down the door of another small room, hoping for a pound or two but never dreaming of the affluence in store.

There was a whole flask of mercury. But right in the middle of the floor of a big, dark closet stood a whole drum of cyanide of potassium not yet unsealed, although the top had been knocked from the crate.

Well; no nugget ever found by a Klondike sourdough or a fossicking old-timer at Ballarat was destined to have more far-reaching results than that unlawful discovery of mine. Like a stone cast into a pool, it has made rings that have not done rippling outward yet.

All I thought of at the time was Grim's need of the stuff, and the probable delight of Jmil Ras, whoever he might be, remembering my own emotions on many an occasion when the needful turned up on a prospect from nowhere. But as the Indians say, we men are only as flies riding on the wheel; we have no foresight worthy of the name; we can guess pretty accurately what will happen when we touch the match to powder; but when a move and a discovery at random fits into the universal scheme so that the whole machinery of nations goes forward half-a-turn, we never dream of the result.

It was enough that Grim had what he wanted. In presence of that satisfaction difficulties vanished, and the business of repacking the stuff into improvised containers that could be hauled up-chimney — of following it with a rope under my armpits that cut like a medieval torture-rack — of rounding up cement and sand in order to reset the grille in place above the chimney — all got accomplished somehow.

Fortunately I had left my Bedouin cloak on the roof, and so could hide the torn and filthy state of my clothes when I reached the street. A good sluicing from a goat-skin water-bag in Ali Baba's camel-*khan* removed the soot from head and hands, and I was able to regain the governorate and get upstairs unnoticed by any one but Grim, who smiled at me through the open door as I passed, but said nothing. De Crespigny's back was turned, which was as well.

Narayan Singh bought new, clean clothes for me in the *suk,* and brought them up to de Crespigny's bedroom; and he smuggled out my sooty rags for some beggar's benefit. I rather expected Grim to come upstairs and ask me questions, but he didn't, and if de Crespigny suspected anything he kept quiet about it too.

Before he left with my discarded clothes Narayan Singh put

my mind at ease about the plunder, and gave me some information on another point that proved important in its way.

"Old Ali Baba has nailed up the poison in new boxes, and is hiding them among the camel-loads, *sahib,* He is in a great good temper, for he swears that you, *sahib,* are a prince of thieves with whom it is an honor to go stealing! He vows that your name shall be no longer Ramsden, but Harami. [Thief] Henceforth he says he is your father and is proud to call you son!"

Chapter VI

"Yemen — a thousand miles away — that hardly sounds like Jeremy!"

So WE WERE a well-found, well-contented party that rode out of El-Kalil that night and headed for the south end of the Dead Sea. Old Ali Baba is as careful of his camels as a good sea captain of his ship, as well as past master at judging their points, which are more elusive than those of a horse but equally important. We were mounted on the best beasts out of Syria, and swayed along at a fine clip under the stars in almost utter silence, except for the half-dozen brass bells swinging from camel's necks. The baggage beasts were tied in strings of four, and each string was towed, as it were, by one of Ali Baba's sons. The rest of us rode anywhere we chose to in the line, with Grim and Ali Baba leading, knee to knee.

We all get our share of knocks and disappointments, but I have found the world a good old ball for all that, and have enjoyed the past, take it on the whole, nearly as much as I expect to like the future. Having wandered, I have seen and experienced a thousand things that are only hearsay to the fellows who have to stand by the home jobs, and there aren't many of the pleasant ways that I haven't sampled. But the best of all were those nights on camel-back, on what Grim calls his beat.

The moonlight made the dusty dry land seem to be carpeted with snow. The deep, blue-velvet shadows seemed to be full of the ghosts of ancient history, and the camel-bells intoned the same tune that has chimed along ridge and wadi, desert and dry water-course for six or seven thousand years that we know about, and only the stars can tell you how many ages before that — each bell sounding a different note. And as no two camels stride alike there is no monotony; the carillon keeps changing.

You don't talk much. Now and then a curt remark is shouted down the line; but for the most part you sit up there and meditate, with your head among the stars — rifle slung behind you — swaying comfortably as the beasts swing forward everlastingly — too contented to talk, or even to smoke.

You'll hear a different tale from folk who have ridden baggage-camels for their sins. There is a great gulf fixed between the two experiences — a gulf as wide as that between old Ali Baba's gang and the thieves who pose as law-abiding men. In a land where ninety-nine percent or so are thieves, it is safest and least mortifying to share your tent and provender with such as call themselves by their right name; frankly admitting that they are rascals — taking open pride in it, in fact — they will frankly find a decent camel for you. That quality of frankness is invariably based on elemental manhood, which is the only thing worth betting on anywhere from West Street to Hoboken, going East.

Nothing happened for four days, until we reached the rusty track of the Hedjaz Railway twenty miles to the southward of El-Maan, not far from where a desert track reaches out toward Petra and the Edom Mountains. There we gave the camels a twenty-four-hour rest after their long climb out of the Jordan Valley; for it doesn't matter how carefully, and with what experience, you cinch the loads, up-hill and down-hill work are going to punish animals that were built for traveling at speed along the level.

So we pitched our little cluster of worn tents in the shade of an enormous rock, and sat down desert-fashion; which means that: we did nothing with both hands continuously, while the camels munched dry thorns the day long and moaned and muttered through the night. We had the loads arranged in a semi-circle like a wall around us, and barring the flies and a scorpion or two, along with rather more sun and hot wind than you get at the seaside, that was as good a place to waste time in as any.

We had forced the camels to one long march in order to reach that spot at nightfall, so as to start off again by night when the full day's rest was over. By four o'clock of the afternoon, a little while before the hot wind died, we all began to grow restless. Mujrim got into an argument with Ali Baba as to whether it wasn't time to go and round up the camels, which started a lecture by the old man, every word of which I had heard ten times before; so I went over to Grim's tent, where he was sitting in the entrance with his legs crossed, smoking.

I hadn't anything particular to say; you seldom do have after the fourth day out, when all the details of the daily routine have arranged themselves and the world you left behind you seems a million miles away. But I'm not as self-contained as Grim — haven't yet quite rid myself of the silly civilized convention which obliges you to say something whenever you approach a man. There's no excuse for it. You're never really fit to be a man's friend until you can let the days go by without a word. Talk, at best, is only a substitute for proper apprehension, as the animals and ancients understand. Grim is always polite, even when you break in on his solitude.

"Strange," I said, "that you can't recall my Australian friend Jeremy. At the time when he was transferred from Egypt for special service under you, Lawrence, I'm told, was holding Petra; and as you were doing factotum for Lawrence, you must have been somewhere between here and Akaba at that time. Doesn't the neighborhood stir your memory? When you return to a place after a considerable absence, don't all the incidents and the people connected with it in your experience come back to mind?"

"Why, yes, they generally do," said Grim.

"Unaccountable, then, that you can't remember him. He was not the kind that is easy to forget — a boisterous, lovable, laughing, handsome fellow, well set up, and as full of tricks as an organ-grinder's monkey — ready with his hands — a great conjurer. Good Lord, man! You couldn't possibly set eyes on Jeremy and not remember him. Did he die before he got to you?"

Grim eyed me steadily for thirty seconds, not considering me, apparently, nor my question, but turning over something in his mind that puzzled him.

"Why do you suppose," he said at last, "that a fellow like Jeremy Ross should choose a country like Arabia to soldier in? Wasn't he fond of company and good jokes? Wasn't Ross the sort of man who whoops her up with the crowd whenever possible, and goes crazy from loneliness?"

"He'd heard of you. He told me his one ambition was to see service under your command. No, I should say Jeremy could burn his own smoke as well as any man."

"You think so? You really think that?" Grim asked me with surprizing earnestness.

"Spill the beans," I suggested. "I never could guess conundrums. Out with what you know."

I BELIEVE IT HURTS Grim almost physically to divulge his thoughts before what seems to him the proper time. It isn't that he can't trust you, for his judgment of whom to trust is more nearly infallible than any man's I know; and he has the courage of his own conviction. Neither does he mistrust himself, or he would never undertake the dangerous missions he delights in. The nearest parallel that I can think of is that of a Scot with money in his purse; he is canny in the use of it, and careful not to tell. When he must, as it were, spend the information he hates not to get value in return for it.

"Your friend Jeremy Ross," he said at last, "was in my camp all told about three weeks. He was a good man, but utterly undisciplined; I should say he was so sure of his own keen intelligence that orders from a less intelligent superior seemed like an insult to him.

"We put him to work at Akaba off-loading cattle out of bumboats, and he doped out a new way of doing it without using gear or injuring the cattle — did a rare good job, in fact. But there was a certain Major Hendrick there, who knew nothing about cattle, but had opinions; and one of his opinions was that Jeremy Ross needed snubbing. So he ordered the method changed.

"It cost us about fifty head of cattle, and Ross said things not provided for in the army regulations. Well, you know how it is; when a trooper talks back at a major, the trooper gets the worst end. I was a major, too, but Hendrick was my senior, and you have to watch points in any case, taking the part of a trooper against an officer. The best I could do was to pretend I knew nothing, and to transfer Ross out of reach for the time being. Major Hendrick proposed to make a court-martial case of it, but there wasn't any place to lock a man up in, and I shipped Ross away with a supply caravan that started inland the same afternoon. Hendrick kicked up an awful row, but couldn't prove that I knew the Australian was under arrest; and anyhow, I was too busy to be quarreled with."

"What did Hendrick do about it?" I asked; for Grim showed symptoms of drying up at the source.

"Nothing. Hendrick died that night. The cattle he didn't understand broke loose and he was horned in the dark. But I guess Ross had the wind up. His defaulter sheet was none too rosy, and a man of his caliber doesn't enjoy the prospect of military prison — especially for an accumulation of alleged offences that are not considered crimes in civil life. Ross disappeared."

"Deserted?"

Grim raised his eyebrows noncommittally. "You couldn't prove it by me. The whole caravan disappeared, and Ross with it. That sort of thing happened rather frequently, because we hadn't officers to spare, and now and then the Arabs used to call it a short war, when left to themselves, and light out for home with any plunder they could lay their hands on. Whether they took Jeremy Ross with them, or killed him before they bolted, didn't transpire."

Bear in mind, Grim wasn't deliberately trying to keep information from me. I'm quite sure of that. I suspect that most of these secret keepers, who get the name for iron self-control, really withhold information just as naturally as they breathe. The self-control in Grim's case is added on to a prenatal peculiarity.

Mujrim and two of his brothers started off after the camels and that was a job that would take them fully half-an-hour. There was plenty of time to coax admissions out of Grim, so I settled down cross-legged straight in front of him and pulled out cigarets.

"Now, see here, Grim," said I, "I knew Jeremy Ross and I know you. You didn't help him out of that scrape for nothing, and he didn't disappear for nothing. No fellow of your disposition could know Jeremy for three weeks and not appreciate him. What did you and he cook up together?"

"Nothing."

"He didn't die and you know it! What became of him?"

"I don't know."

"You mean you've no official knowledge!"

"Well?"

"Who's this Jmil Ras we're going to see?"

"We're going to see."

"Jmil Ras — Jeremy Ross — I've heard names more dissimilar! Are they one and the same man?"

"Wait and see," he answered, smiling at me blandly.

"You've no call to be reserved with me," I said. "Even if you did connive at Jeremy's desertion, and admitted it to me, I wouldn't give you away. Surely you know that?"

He nodded. "I didn't. I've no proof that he deserted, and I don't believe he did. I don't know a thing about him for certain."

"What do you know about Jmil Ras?"

"No more, and no less than I know about Jeremy Ross."

"Then what do you suspect?"

"That's different."

"Spill it!"

"About a dozen incidents since the armistice was signed have led me to suspect that Jeremy Ross wasn't killed. I hardly believed at the time that he could have been — at all events, not by the men he went away with that afternoon. He was clowning, ventriloquizing, and doing stunts for them before they started; and you've no notion how the Arabs idolize a fellow who can do that kind of thing. He had a natural gift for learning Arabic, and a talent for amusing folk that was even greater than his flair for resenting Jack-in-officiousness; and underneath all that he had keen common sense. There was nothing the matter with Jeremy Ross except boisterous spirits and a little too much independence."

"And you're pretty sure in your own mind — aren't you? — that Jmil Ras and Jeremy Ross are the same."

"I won't say that. It's just possible; and I've known of equally strange circumstances. It might be the worst that could have happened, if it's true."

"How so?"

"This message from the Avenger doesn't look good. If Jeremy Ross can really burn his own smoke, as you called it just now; and if Jmil Ras is really he, we may be able to pull a fat chestnut out of the fire for Feisul. But if Jmil Ras is a Jeremy Ross who got bored and lost patience, then all these supplies we're taking him will only add fuel to the fire. I wouldn't help Jeremy Ross or any other white man exploit Arabia against the Arabs. I'm for the Arabs in their own country, and dead set against all foreign interference. However, it may all turn out to be a mare's nest. We'll know soon."

There were other matters to learn first, though, and one was how fast the post can ride when Arabia deigns to admit she is in a hurry. Why is it that the men who drive like Jehu son of Nimshi are the most lethargic at all other times? Your consistently energetic man hardly ever drives furiously.

There came a rider like a black insect in a dust-cloud, pushing a racing camel as if life depended on the number of yards covered before dark. We could see the incessant stick long before we could make out whether we were to be spoken with or avoided; in fact, the rider was in such a hurry that we were possibly unseen in the shadow of that great acre of rock until we were so close that a rifle shot could have compelled an interview.

It was no man, but a woman, dressed in the somber black cotton from head to foot that usually hides the Bedouin lady's charms; and the moment she was near enough to recognize us she gave a wild, shrill cry of welcome that put at rest all doubt of her intention and of her identity.

She cried out again when Grim got to his feet, and rode at him like a warrior brandishing her rifle.

But none raised a rifle to prevent her. We all knew Ayisha, the divorced wife of Ali Higg the self-styled Lion of Petra, whom Grim had managed to remarry to Saoud the Avenger. I told about that in the last tale. She was the last person in the world who would want to injure Grim. Besides, she was laughing.

And Lord! Wasn't she good to look at, as she halted her spent beast within a yard of him, saluting with her hand up to her forehead like a man. Most of those desert women grow old early, and are hags at twenty-eight. She was possibly twenty, or twenty-one, and though she must have been nearly as tired as the camel, she looked seventeen and shone with youth through the mask of desert dust.

"*Il awafi!* [Hail] O, Jimgrim, it is good to see you!" she exclaimed, laughing down at him before leaping from the camel to stand facing him as frankly as a woman from the West. She had learned a lot from her short association with us at the time Grim checkmated Ali Higg, being one of those rare Eastern women who learn quickly because they are not too conservatively settled in the ancient ways.

"Welcome, Ayisha! What brings you?" Grim answered smiling.

"An ill-wind brings me! Thanks to the Lord of Mercies who sent you to befriend me, Jimgrim, I have a man for husband. But Allah jests savagely now and then."

"Are the other wives too jealous of you?" Grim asked; for there wasn't any other likely reason why a rather newly married woman should be riding away from home alone in all that hurry.

"No," she answered. "Not too jealous. Not more than enough to amuse me. But unless you come swiftly I am like to lose my man!"

The camels were collected in a bunch and were roaring out their usual objections to being saddled and put to work; but instead of swearing back at them and putting on the harness all our gang had come clustering around Grim and Ayisha. But Narayan Singh came thrusting himself among them, elbowing right and left.

"Are ye cattle or men?" he thundered. "Is there no room to spread in all this desert? Is there no work to do? Ye cluster like the flies around a bad smell, yet ye have enough smell of your own to shame a camel, every one of you!"

That was hardly a gentle hint, but they seemed disinclined to take it. Moreover, they weren't a good gang to insult too freely — not if you hoped to preserve peace. I was as keen as any one to hear what Ayisha had to say, but it was likely that if I waited they would all stay too, and Narayan Singh might feel the point of a long knife for his trouble. So I led the way toward the camels and lent a hand with the heaviest loads — a task that even Mujrim, their strongest, was pleased enough to have me perform.

So I got no other information just then than the guess-work of the gang tossed off between grunts, as they saddled the protesting camels, with all the assurance with which old-timers pretend they know when they don't, the wide world over. Mujrim pretended to know most, of course, since he had paid a secret visit to Jmil Ras; and the whole-cloth completeness of his misinformation may explain why Grim hadn't bothered as much as to question him about the man whose goods we were delivering.

"Jmil Ras is a handsome Sheik, whose wives are growing old. He has seen Ayisha, and she him. Her husband the Avenger is jealous, for he is a proud Sheik, to whom it is no pleasure to consider sharing his fourth wife with a rival; so he set a strong guard to close the road between Ayisha and Jmil Ras. But he who would keep a she-fox in the ground should stop the hole at both ends! He watches that way, and she has bolted this. She heard that our Jimgrim is coming, and ran to meet him! Can not he who married her to the Avenger marry her again to Jmil Ras? That is the long and short of it. Look — see how she pleads with him there where they stand together."

Ali Baba, for very pride in his great black-bearded oldest-born, confirmed every word of that story. He was in position to, of course, not having visited Jmil Ras, nor having anything to go on but imagination. Supposing Jmil Ras really to be Jeremy, I could have invented that sort of story all too easily myself, and was only too prone to believe it; for a man doesn't need to have Jeremy's fondness for company before he can get into trouble with women, in a land where that kind of thing is deadly dangerous. I could very easily imagine Jeremy indulging in an affair with Ayisha, just out of devilment and for the sake of running counter to convention.

Before we had got the camels loaded there were raw jokes going the round, and the whole gang was set for a romance in high life, with daggers, poison, torture, and a couple of blood-feuds all thrown in — enjoying the prospect almost as much as if it were something that had actually happened, for Mahommed, the gang poet, to make songs about. For they prefer to glorify with song the past that all men know, rather than the future that lies in Allah's lap.

And though Narayan Singh affected to attach no weight to their prognostications, his own were hardly reassuring. He and I sat on the rump of a loaded camel, smoking and watching Grim, waiting for him to give the order to march.

"Hitherto we had a problem that was simple," he growled. "What it was I know not, but it was simple, for it had to do with men. Now there is a woman in it, and nothing that they touch is simple any longer. Moreover, we know the woman. What is worse, she knows us. Those women remember things that a man forgets; and if one of us in the past once showed a weakness, she will use that as a target for her brains at every opportunity."

"She is grateful to Jimgrim," I answered. "It isn't likely she would try to injure us."

"No woman knows what is injury to a man," he retorted. "Whatever looks good to her, she believes must be good for her victims. I knew a woman once who truly thought that death must be good for me because she wished to see me dead; she was a very religious woman and a great advocate of reform among us Sikhs, but I observed that the changes she proposed were all designed for her advantage. She wished to see me dead because of things I knew that she did not wish known. So I made love to her, and she drank the poison she prepared for me. I shall make strong love to Ayisha; it is safest."

He had made what he calls "strong love" to her right up to the day when Grim contrived to marry her to the Avenger, but hadn't accomplished much beyond providing her and all the rest of us with amusement by the way. I dare say I grinned reminiscently.

"You have my permission to laugh at me," he said, "for you are one of those who laugh without contempt and jest without malice. Nevertheless, it is better to be like Jimgrim and not laugh when a man speaks out of his heart's knowledge. Ayisha will make show of scorning my advances, but I shall make all the more show of over-whelming passion. To her that will seem like a weakness. And as in war we look for the enemy's weak point, so she, being a woman, will look for this party's weakest member and will suppose that I am the one. Thus, whatever her purpose may be, she will try to use me. I shall seem to walk into her trap, with the result that Jimgrim will receive what the army calls intelligence."

Well, it looked to me rather like a bear-trap set to catch a fly, but there never was sense in sneering at an honest fellow's notions. I changed the subject slightly.

"What do you suppose is the reason why the Avenger has sent for Jimgrim?"

"As well try to guess what is behind the moon! But I know this, *sahib*, and you know it too, for you were present. It was agreed between Jimgrim and the Avenger that because the Avenger yielded to Jimgrim's terms of settlement in the Ali Higg dispute, when he might easily have broken faith and made great trouble, therefore the Avenger should have the right to send for Jimgrim to help him out of any difficulty.

"And the Avenger said — you heard him say it — that if there should be no excuse for summoning Jimgrim he would take care to create one. Well, *sahib*, if you give a child a pistol he will fire it off. These Arabs are children, and the most like children are the chiefs, for they have men's lives to play with, which are the most enticing toys. Give an Arab chief the right to send for such a man as Jimgrim whenever he gets into trouble, and he will make trouble. The nature of the trouble? Who knows? Who cares? Trouble is the name of it. It is all one. You will find that our Jimgrim has his work cut out."

The sun was nearly down by then, and the gang cook — one of Ali Baba's grandsons — spilled hot rice, coconut oil, and rubbery chicken into a great tin pan, around which we squatted on our hunkers for the evening meal, Narayan Singh foregoing all the rules of caste — as the Sikh is supposed to do in any case, but almost never does, except at the spur of necessity. We dipped our right hands into the mess and ate in the usual hurry, because whoever doesn't eat fast gets a lot less than his share.

But Grim ate alone. And Ayisha ate alone; for not even her disrespect for convention entitled her to share a meal with menfolk. It was really a remarkable concession that she wasn't kept waiting until after we had finished; and it wouldn't have been made, only that Grim was determined on an early start.

Most of us were stanch Moslems, and those who were not were pretending to be, but the law requiring prayer at sunset, which is all-important, was forgotten, whereas there was quite a little comment on the circumstance that the *bint*, as they called Ayisha, was allowed to give herself such airs. In fact, we acted pretty much like Christians, take us on the whole.

I didn't get a chance to talk to Grim until we had left the camping-place a mile behind and were heading nearly southeast over wilderness that Moses and his horde made famous centuries ago. Then I whacked my camel to a gallop and drew beside him in the lead.

"Well; what's the news?" I asked him, for it was a dead sure bet that he wouldn't tell me unless I did ask.

"Jmil Ras came from Yemen at the south end of Arabia about two years ago. He has a ragtag following, said to be very fierce and rather well-disciplined; and he has established himself in a deserted village on the side of a hill about twenty miles from Abu Kem, where he defies all comers.

"They say he has rebuilt the village and fortified it strongly, and the malcontents are flocking from all over the place to join him. The Avenger, who claims to rule that district, demanded tribute, which was scornfully refused. The Avenger threatened to exterminate him, and Jmil Ras retorted by ambushing about a hundred of the Avenger's men, taking their camels and weapons, stripping them, and sending them back stark naked with a verbal message to the general effect that two can play at the extermination game. So the Avenger has sent for me."

"But why Ayisha?"

"The man who brought the message to Jerusalem seems to have disappeared. Nothing's been heard of him. Most likely he was murdered for his camel and rifle. The Avenger had relays of men in wait at different points to intercept him and pass the word along. They've seen us and reported us by signal; so Ayisha was sent to meet us half way on the supposition that possibly the first messenger never reached Jerusalem. It seems she told the Avenger she has influence with me; and his other wives encouraged him to send her off alone so as to have a good basis for starting an intrigue against her."

"Yemen?" I said. "That's a thousand miles away. That hardly sounds like Jeremy."

"No," he admitted, "it hardly does. But then there's this — they say Jmil Ras is a magician, who can change bullets into gold and make the dead saints talk in their tombs. Does that sound to you like an Arab, or an impudently humorous Australian?"

Chapter VII

"A member of a strangely free and independent, brave and disrespectful sect."

I GOT NO MORE out of Grim. He did not propose to hamper his free range of thought with guesswork based on half the facts, and said so. I believe that on such occasions he forces his thoughts into channels that lead anywhere at all except into the maze that lies ahead of him — thinks about the stars, or cabbages and kings, or Shakespeare.

Maybe I'm wrong about that; but I know that when we halted about midnight for a half-hour rest and I drew abreast of him again, he pulled out a pocket edition of Mark Twain — *A Yankee at King Arthur's Court* I think it was — and leaned against his camel's rump to read it in the moonlight.

Perhaps it was only a hint to me that he didn't want to talk, but I think not. He seemed really absorbed in the book, wrinkling his forehead over the fine print and chuckling occasionally, very quietly, as if the humor were a secret between the author and himself.

Our Arabs were hugely impressed. Ali Baba beckoned me away, and I joined him, thinking he had some request to make to Grim by proxy. When the old fox had any particularly outrageous demand in mind he usually tried to make me the go-between, partly because Grim seldom refused me anything if he could help it, but also in order to lay the blame of a possible refusal on to my head and retain the good opinion of his sons, who regarded him as an arch-strategist, who could always get what he wanted. However, for a wonder, he had no request to pass along on that occasion.

"Jimgrim prays," he said sternly. "Let him alone. I have talked with the woman Ayisha. Sometimes women don't lie, and if the tenth of what she says is true it will take a deal of prayer to get us through to Jmil Ras."

As he was a professional thief, and all his sons and grandsons were the same, I was curious to know exactly why that thought should trouble him.

"You've had your money, haven't you?" said I. "If you can't get through, what difference does it make?"

He stroked his beard for thirty seconds before answering, and his wrinkled old face grew reproachful.

"In El-Kalil," he said at last, with something near grief in his voice, "I named you Harami, but you are Ramsden after all! Under that black beard of yours is only a fool's face, or you wouldn't ask such a question. Under that great strength is only a sheep's heart. You will never make an honest thief! *Bismillah!* Ask my sons; ask Mujrim — ask Mahommed — Hassan — Achmet — Yussuf — any one of them. Ask what I would do to any one of them who named a price and took the pay but failed to keep faith! You have no understanding, Ramsden; you are only a foreign unbeliever with the strength and the brains of a bull! Jimgrim would never ask such a question. Not even that bull-headed Sikh would ask it. Allah! Am I to be thought a common cheat in my old age?"

How was that for a rebuke? I called him Allah's pet rascal and tried to jolly him out of his ill temper, but he was as ruffled as a turkey in the wind, and the more I sought to soothe him the angrier he became. So I told him I would forgive him if he liked for that good repeating pistol of mine that he stole on our former trip and, quoting a text from the Koran about unseemly pride, left him to think that over.

It hurts loaded camels to stand still, and our beasts were all kneeling, grumbling of course, and squealing for a bite at any one who passed them close enough. I went and squatted beside Mujrim in the lee of one of them, for he and I had been great friends ever since I fought and licked him in the Valley of Moses close to Petra. He nodded in the direction of his irascible old father, as much as to say that I wasn't the only one who got into a bath of anger now and then, but said nothing, and warned me with a gesture to keep silence too.

There were voices coming from the far side of the camel next to us — Narayan Singh's deep bass, and Ayisha's alto. I suppose you couldn't choose a more suitable scene for making love, with the moonlight bathing the desert in honey-colored light, colored stars twinkling almost close enough to be plucked like jewels from a purple pall, and the hills on the horizon looming softly mysterious, sending the vague, spicy scent of Araby toward us on a warm wind.

"O darling!" boomed the Sikh in his best Arabic, that is perfectly grammatical but contains a softer, throatier aspirate than any Arab can accomplish. "O heart of my desire! What does it matter to me that a son of sixty dogs who dubs himself Avenger flatters himself by calling you his fourth wife? I am a Pathan of the Orakzai — a man of violence, whose passion brooks no living rival!"

"You mean you are a pig from the Indian hills?" she suggested without audible emotion.

"Nay, beloved, I mean this: That as I said a thousand times before I say again, I will pull kings off their thrones and fill dry wells with their carcasses until there are no more kings to stand between me and my heart's desire; but cease I never will until you admit you are mine!"

"Until the moon falls out of the sky then!"

"What are the doings of the moon to me!" the Sikh retorted scornfully. "Let him [the moon is masculine in Hindu mythology] fall, and we shall have good darkness for great deeds! You shall be mine, whatever happens to the moon!"

"Bukra fil mishmish!" [Literally, "tomorrow there will be apricots." An Arab proverb referring to a princess, who put off a disagreeable suitor from day to day by promising to marry him when the apricots were ripe; but each night she plucked the ripe ones from the tree.] she quoted, laughing. It was clear that she was at least amused by his protestations.

"What need have we of moons when two eyes such as thine can burn up night?" he boomed. "I shall see to fight by their radiance! I will make you a necklace out of the milk-white teeth of emperors whom I shall slay for your sake, and all the women in the world shall squint with jealousy! Consider a while, beloved — did I not swear to you before that I would come again to find you? Here I am!"

"Here to clean the boots of Jimgrim," she suggested.

"Here in obedience to Destiny!"

He almost said Karma, but remembered in the nick of time not to use the Hindu term. Not that it would have mattered, for she wouldn't have understood what Karma meant.

"And here art thou, O heart's desire, also at the call of that same Destiny! But you doubt?"

"Surely!"

"Put me to a test then! Come! Let us make a plan together. We Orakzai Pathans are good at plans, and better yet at forcing them through broken teeth down the throats of the fools who oppose us! How about this Avenger now, who thinks he owns you? Shall we make a corpse of him and claim his heritage? How would you like to be queen of this part of Arabia for a beginning — just for a beginning?"

She answered with a low laugh, no such fool as to believe a word of it, but nevertheless delighted; for immeasurable though a man's desire may be, it is at least a compliment that he should seek to give his lady-love a glimpse of it; and where there is all that smoke an element of fire lies underneath. And who should blame a woman of that incorrigible land who took advantage of a such vainglorious boaster?

HOWEVER, THAT WAS as far as the intrigue could go just then, for Grim's whistle announced that time was up. Ayisha mounted behind me, because her own beast was hardly in fit condition to be towed, so furiously had she ridden to meet Grim. I did not invite her on to my beast, but I put my foot on his neck and swung into the saddle as he rose, and she vaulted up behind me with a rifle in her right hand — not such an easy feat by a long way as it looks on paper.

She knew Grim was an American, but I suppose she had no reason for suspecting me; and maybe I had learned the part of an educated Indian from Lahore fairly well by that time. I couldn't have fooled another Indian for a minute, but her native shrewdness wasn't experienced enough to detect any slight mistakes I made from time to time.

And it is a peculiarity of that land that however strong, influential, wealthy or even courageous an Indian may be, the Bedouins regard him as an inferior, whether Moslem or not. Our seventeen thieves were not Bedouins, but men of El-Kalil, who hold themselves superior to Bedouin and Fellahin alike — superior, in fact, to all Eastern peoples and the equals of the conquering white; they drew no such social distinction, and judged men more by personal merit.

They knew me for an American and a trusted friend of Grim, who had beaten their champion Mujrim in fair fight; and they recognized in Narayan Singh a Sikh, who was also Grim's friend, and a man of parts. But Ayisha knew no such standards of comparison as they, and her attitude toward me was that of a duchess to her confidential butler — if you can imagine a dusty duchess in black cotton, with a rifle in one hand, jumping up on to the butler's camel.

I was at a disadvantage, having her behind me. I like to watch the face of anyone I'm talking to, the study of faces being a hobby of mine that I have found as expensive in the long run and as profitable in the end as collecting postage stamps or curios. For it takes you a long time to learn what shades of expression mean, and as you back your judgment you pay accordingly; but what you do learn finally can't be found in books or filched from you by competitors.

She put her left hand over my left shoulder, ostensibly to keep her balance, although she needed that as much as a cat needs crutches on a wall. It was a shapely, slender hand with henna'd nails, and there was a ring on the middle finger with an uncut sapphire set in it that I dare say would bring two or three thousand dollars on Fifth Avenue. I didn't pay much attention to it until the fingers began tugging at my whiskers that were growing black and unkempt after nearly a week without shaving. It isn't considered complimentary to play tricks with a man's beard in Moslem lands, but I let that pass. She tugged until I turned my face half around toward her before she spoke.

"O *Miyan*," she said then, using the rather contemptuous term by which they address all Indians, "you are a doctor, for I have seen you use the knife and give the physic. How much magic do you know? All *Miyan*s know magic."

It was true I had charge of the medicine-chest, but if ever there was an unqualified surgeon or physician, I am he. I can skin a dead beast, having had experience of that; and when it comes to lancing boils or opening an abscess with a safety-razor blade, I have the stomach for it and can cut deep. But I give copious castor-oil for all complaints, and am seldom twice in demand by the same patient. As for magic — my hands are calloused and not subtle; I can't even shuffle a pack of cards without making a hopeless mess of it. But it doesn't always pay to confess ignorance, unless you're sure of being found out.

"I know magic when I see it. There is magic in your eyes, O lady Ayisha," I answered guardedly. It is generally pretty safe to pay a compliment when you haven't any other answer ready.

"To whom are you taking all this baggage?" she demanded next.

Only the enfranchised woman sticks to what a man considers is the point; but I've noticed that the female sex does keep a point in mind as a general rule, for all that, and I answered guardedly again —

"Ask Jimgrim."

"Bah! As well ask the desert! Jimgrim listens and never speaks. I asked one of Ali Baba's sons, and he said the goods are for some one on a mountain-side. He thought that a clever answer. Jmil Ras lives on a mountain-side; are the goods for him?"

"They are not my goods," I answered. "How should I know? I go wherever Jimgrim leads." And thinking to turn the tables on her I asked a question, "Who is Jmil Ras?"

"Jmil Ras is a great magician. I know the goods are for him."

"Some people know what isn't true. How do you know?"

"Because it is known that that oaf Mujrim came and went, escaping the Avenger's men by the thickness of the shadow of his camel's smell. If they had caught him, he would have been made to talk; but spies were sent after him, and it is known that Ali Baba began buying goods at once in El-Kalil. Were the goods not for Jmil Ras?"

"How should I know?"

"*Malaish!* The Avenger will take the goods. None can prevent, for he lies between here and the mountain where Jmil Ras has entrenched himself."

"Entrenched?" said I.

"He has dug great ditches. Is there magic among these camel-loads?"

I thought of the quicksilver. Whoever has used that stuff as much as I have, and seen it absorb the gold out of broken quartz, may be forgiven for talking like an old-time alchemist.

"Magic?" said I. "Woman, there is stuff among those loads that at a word from me will either poison the very devils in the pit or turn rocks into money! It is metal, and yet it runs to and fro like water; it is liquid, and yet so heavy that it sinks like lead and will not mix with water! It shines like burnished silver, yet can not be coined; and a drop of it will make the teeth fall from the jaws of a giant!"

"That is good stuff," she answered. "Give me some of it!"

You'll have full right to laugh at me, you fellows, if you see fit, after you have ridden camel-back under the stars with a pretty girl's hand on your shoulder, her breath in your ear, and her soft voice coaxing you. I'm no Don Juan, nor no Saint Anthony — merely a fellow who has had that rare experience. You may take it from me unreservedly that there are circumstances and conditions in which it is easier to keep your head and to refuse requests.

"What do you want it for?" I countered.

"It is enough that I do want it. Am not I, Ayisha, your friend of old?"

I laughed at that. "You're the woman," said I, "who stuck a knife into my leg when I was fighting Mujrim!"

"Oh, as for that — *malaish!*" she answered. "That is a little thing forgotten. Has the wound not healed?"

"There is only a scar there now," I assured her. "Do you recognize all your friends by the dagger-marks you make on them?"

Her answer to that was unexpected, even if characteristic. She withdrew her left hand, and in less than half a second I could feel her dagger's point against my ribs.

"Now, *Miyan!*" she exclaimed with a hard little laugh. "I need thy magic! Does life seem sweet?"

"The magic won't work without me to give it orders," I retorted, trying to speak evenly; but that dagger-point tickled as well as pricked.

She pushed it in a fraction of an inch, and the thing was getting beyond a joke.

"Give it your orders, then, *Miyan!* Put a piece of it in my hand and tell it to obey me!"

"It is necessary first to make a spell," said I. "Unless I wave my arms to summon devils the magic won't work."

"Summon them!"

She pricked me again with the dagger to emphasize her authority, and I think she was rather surprized that an Indian should act as I did then. Did you ever try acrobatic stunts on the back of a pacing camel? It was my first attempt at anything of that sort, but she was at a disadvantage too, in that her perch was even less secure than mine. I spread both arms outward to their full extent, as if to summon devils from all corners of the universe — leaned back, face upward, as if praying to the stars — seized her suddenly by neck and shoulders — and yanked her, heels over head, into my lap so suddenly that she had not even time to drop her rifle or drive the dagger into me.

Having her in both arms then it was a comparatively easy task to take the dagger away, although she bit until her teeth met in my arm; and when I loosed her a little to let her breathe she tried to use the rifle as a club to brain me with.

Meanwhile, the camel didn't help matters in the least. He objected to acrobatics, and from the way he carried on all the devils I was supposed to have been summoning might have been torturing his stomach. When Narayan Singh rode close and seized the head-rope the silly brute pulled backward trying to jerk his own head off, and kicked out at random, north, south, east and west. However, we got going again; but by that time I brought up the rear of the procession, with Narayan Singh acting escort on the left flank.

"Now, you little cannibal," said I at last, "suppose you tell me what you want that magic for!"

"Wait till I turn the Avenger loose on you!" she panted.

"All right," I said, "I'll wait. Meanwhile, let's go forward and talk with Jimgrim."

If Grim was at all aware of what had been happening, he made no sign. It wasn't unusual for a camel somewhere in the line to start squealing and fighting, and no one took much notice as a rule unless he happened to be too close to the brute's teeth. Grim, away off in the lead, might easily have failed to notice the disturbance. Ayisha did not propose that he should learn the details of it now.

"Peace, *Miyan!*" she exclaimed, trying to laugh. "I was only joking."

"Next time you joke, then, do it with your lips, and keep your dagger and teeth for eating with!" said I.

"Give me back the dagger."

Instead, I whistled and tossed it to Narayan Singh, who caught it deftly by the hilt. She shuddered when I whistled, for most Arabs and all Bedouins regard that as the devil's music.

"The Pathan shall keep it for a love-token," I said. "Men of his race would rather have that sort of thing than a kiss. Come on, now, tell me what you wanted magic for!"

But instead of answering my question, she called to her amorous Pathan in the strange, reverberating voice with which Eastern women have spurred their men to fight ever since Cain killed Abel.

"Come closer, if you love me! Come and stick that dagger into this fool! Quick! It is the test!"

I had dropped my riding-stick in the scuffle when I yanked her from behind me, and a camel doesn't officially recognize any other accelerator; yet flight was obviously the only way to save the

Sikh from a predicament. He couldn't very well pretend to try to kill me without making himself ridiculous, nor refuse without swallowing his boasts. So I tried to make the beast gallop by kicking and swearing at him, which works occasionally.

But Narayan Singh saw the same way out of the predicament that I did. He circled about and approached from the rear, as if intending to stab me in the back; but it was my camel's rump that stopped the dagger-point, and no new-fangled racing auto ever leapt into speed more suddenly than that ill-used, ill-tempered mount of mine.

We had overtaken Grim in less than sixty seconds, with the Sikh still brandishing the dagger two lengths in the rear, and to keep up appearances I claimed Grim's protection. So did she, and Grim transferred her to his camel, which gave Narayan Singh enough excuse to fall to the rear again.

Grim is not given to overlooking bets. He is fonder of listening than of asking questions, and he likes to let events explain themselves rather than render them obscure by being too inquisitive. But not even an Arab could resent interrogation in those circumstances. He held her in his lap the same way I had done, with a quiet eye on her rifle to make sure she should take no pot-shot at me, and without halting — because then old Ali Baba and the gang would all have swarmed about us — asked for my explanation first.

He might as well have wanted pudding before soup, or a seat at a show without the ticket. it couldn't be done.

"Jimgrim," she interrupted, "why do you travel with two miserable Indians? Ali Baba and his men are bad enough, but the other two creatures put you to open shame! Take my rifle and shoot that fool, or else let me do it!"

The moon glistened on their faces, and he smiled at her exactly as if she were a child.

"That *Miyan* there," she went on, "can make magic. He says he has stuff hidden among the loads that will turn the mountains into money and make men's teeth fall out. Kill him before he makes magic against you and me; then we will take his stuff and send Jmil Ras some food that has been treated with it. When that is done, we will turn Abu Kem into money and bribe the British to go away from Palestine Then we will kill all the Jews, and Saoud the Avenger shall be king in Jerusalem. I will poison his other wives, and I shall be a great queen."

"Suppose instead of that we make the *Miyan* work for us?" he suggested kindly. "I don't know how to use that magic stuff of his. Do you?"

"Give him the bastinado then! Make him obedient! He is much too impudent and independent for a *Miyan!*" she insisted.

"That is because he knows magic perhaps. All magicians are proud. Besides," he added, smiling again, "I never bastinado anyone in advance. What were you and he quarreling about?"

"I told you. I want some of his magic."

"What for?"

"To poison Jmil Ras."

"Why?"

"I hate him!"

"What harm has he done you?"

"He has set himself up against my husband the Avenger," she answered, but not very promptly; there was a distinct pause while she considered what answer to make, and Grim noticed it all right.

"They say Jmil Ras is rather young and handsome," he answered. "They also say he has ability, and isn't married. Now, if he were to overthrow the Avenger, he might consider marriage with the youngest and best-looking of the Avenger's wives. Isn't that so?"

"What of it?"

"I am wondering why you should hate him so much in the circumstances."

"I hate him because he is more insolent than this Indian *Miyan* of yours!"

"You spoke with him, and he insulted you?"

"No. How should I speak with him?"

"You have seen him, though?"

"Yes."

"Now let's have that all over again. Jmil Ras is good-looking and unmarried. He is clever, and you say he has set himself up against the Avenger, who is sufficiently afraid of him to send for me. Have you ever sent Jmil Ras any messages?"

She did not answer.

"Has it ever occurred to you, Ayisha, that your position as the Avenger's fourth wife is perhaps a little insecure?"

"It was you, Jimgrim, who arranged my marriage to him; you ought to know."

"Let me see — I think you can't write, can you?"

"No."

"That makes it awkward, doesn't it. People who have to send

messages by word of mouth are sometimes at the mercy of the messenger, eh? The Avenger sent you to me, so I take it he doesn't suspect yet that you've been communicating with Jmil Ras. But I suspect it!"

"You would suspect the Prophet of Al-Islam!" she retorted.

"That may be," he answered, smiling. "He was a great man, but I'm familiar with his history. He and Julius Caesar and Napoleon were all on the watch for opportunity. Now, I'm not blaming you, Ayisha, for I know some of the circumstances; but if you want me to help you as I did once before, hadn't you better take me into your confidence?"

"That *Miyan* is listening."

"He's a magician. Perhaps he could find out what you know in any case. Better not run the risk of his using that magic of his. Didn't you offer to help Jmil Ras if he would marry you?"

I expect the accuracy of Grim's deduction seemed pretty much like magic to her. Add to that the fact that he had helped her once before in dire extremity — his almost tender friendliness — the comfort of being held in the arms of a man with such a name as Jimgrim had earned for keeping other people's confidences — then moonlight, and the whole romantic scene — and it would have been a wonder if she hadn't 'fessed up.

"It was Ibrahim ben Ah," she admitted suddenly, rushing the story now, to get it over and done with.

"The old warrior who commanded the camel-corps of Ali Higg of Petra?"

"Yes. He deserted to the Avenger, but wasn't treated with sufficient dignity, so he deserted again to Jmil Ras. Before he went away he talked with me. *Wallahi!* It was his fault. He swore he would make Jmil Ras a great one, and that if I would persuade the Avenger's men to desert to Jmil Ras, he, Ibrahim ben Ah, would guarantee on his honor that I should be the first wife of Jmil Ras when the time came. So I agreed. But Jmil Ras sent me word by the mouth of a wife of one of his men that he would have nothing to do with any such arrangement — may Allah change his face!"

"And had you already persuaded any of the Avenger's men to desert?"

"No. I had had no opportunity. Jmil Ras had the impudence to tell that woman to tell me to mind my own business! May Allah turn him into worms! I will teach him to despise me!"

Grim glanced in my direction.

"Does he sound like an Arab to you?" he asked.

"Or an Australian?" said I.

"What is an Australian?" Ayisha demanded.

"A member of a strangely free and independent, brave and disrespectful sect," Grim answered, smiling pleasantly.

Chapter VIII

"Miyan, you are a great magician!"

THAT DAWN WE BIVOUACKED in a *fiumara*, which, as I think I have explained before, is a formation peculiar to that country — part valley; part dry river-bed — a roaring torrent for a few days in the year, and all the rest of the time a waste of sand and boulders with a muddy water-hole or two at distant intervals.

They wander across the land snake-fashion, roughly east and west, and what with the banks being high in places, so that men and camels can lie hidden, and the all-important water, they play no inconsiderable part in tribal warfare, which is endemic and deadly.

The water-holes being so scarce, the places where they are known to be are almost like a crossroads, and the hoof and human footprints give an erroneous suggestion of incessant traffic on a large scale. But traffic is actually scarce, no man being fool enough to travel except at the spur of need, since whatever superior force catches sight of a smaller one will certainly pursue and plunder, if not murder.

But being by that time near the indefinite boundary line of the ruling chief whom we were visiting by invitation, we pitched the little tents in an elbow of the *fiumara* near a water-hole without much anxiety, taking no more precaution than to post one man on either bank as soon as we had eaten breakfast, or supper, whichever you like to call the meal after a night march. And I'm fairly well convinced that both men fell asleep within five minutes, although they managed it sitting upright.

Grim went to sleep serenely in his tent, after putting Narayan Singh in charge, who was to make over in turn to me at the end of four hours; and it was the Sikh's military instinct that saved us from ridicule, if nothing worse, and enabled us to turn the tables on fortune.

Within the length of a furlong there the *fiumara* curved exactly like the figure **S**, but there were so many bleached white boulders just above the spot where we pitched that the bed was impracticable, and any one using the course for a road would be obliged to climb out and make a detour, unless he cared to risk breaking a camel's legs.

I don't think Narayan Singh heard anything. He was just so trained in military ways, and so suspicious of new ground that he couldn't keep still. He came and shook me awake at the end of fifteen minutes instead of four hours, and instead of swearing at him, as I had indubitable right to do, based on inviolable custom, I sat up and laughed at the chorus of snores rising up to heaven from our bivouac like the music of a sawmill.

Grim, in the tent next mine, was snoring as loud as any one; and the camels fifty yards away were making a weird row of their own; for, having only one more march ahead of us, we had fed them the remaining corn, and I suppose they thought they were singing songs. You never heard such a trombone-voiced menagerie.

When I had done laughing and had lit a cigaret, my friend the Sikh saw fit to explain himself.

"Even hogs need watching, *sahib!* Look at them! Some lie belly-upward, others belly-down, but it is all one whether a knife strikes before or behind. The hog dies when his blood flows."

"I've heard you snore a time or two!" I answered.

"That is as maybe. Did you hear our Jimgrim put me in charge of this nightmare for four hours?"

"I did. The job's yours. I'm not stealing it!"

"You heard, eh? Then you admit that my honor is involved? Well and good. Come and help me scout for a stone-throw or two."

"Why? Are you afraid of ghosts?" I asked him.

"Neither of us two are men to whom fear should be lightly imputed," he answered. "But call me an old woman if you will. Only come and scout with me. I have an intuition."

Well, I believe in intuitions. I have had them. I believe that if a man can only school himself to follow intuition and not be turned aside by second thoughts or other folks' opinions, he will be as safe in all circumstances as a dollar in. the U.S. Treasury. I put up no further argument, but rose with a yawn and followed him. Now I would have taken to the high bank, being naturally lazy and averse to scrambling over rough rocks when a shorter, smoother trail will serve. But the Sikh led straight on up the winding *fiumara,* and, when we reached the roughest maze of boulders, added difficulty on to inconvenience by warning me to make no noise. For all my size and weight I can go quietly when I choose, having learned that lesson painfully when stalking game for the pot in many hot lands.

And a Sikh, of course, can make less noise than a shadow, as the Germans discovered in Flanders. We could have been seen from above quite easily, but not from in front, for we kept cover behind the stones as we advanced; and I think few animals, and no man not deliberately laying for us, would have heard a sound.

The whole performance smacked more and more of the ridiculous to me, as we crawled around the turns and peered, and saw nothing but jumbled up white rocks. But Narayan Singh was set on his self-appointed task like a cheetah that winds black buck, and he never paused for more than a second or two to make sure.

Most men can learn to scout slowly, but that fellow can go unseen over rough ground nearly as fast as a man walks on the level, and keeping up with him was no joke. We came within ten yards of a small panther and surprized him out of his sleep, which may give some idea of how much noise we made.

But nothing whatever happened, except that the panther spat at us and hesitated for a moment whether to show fight or run, until we reached the last bend of the figure **S** and could see nearly straight ahead up the bed of the *fiumara* for maybe half a mile. Then Narayan Singh, who was about two lengths ahead of me, suddenly lay quite flat, and whispered.

"Kabadar!" ["Take care!"]

I crawled up beside him, and he didn't know I was there until he turned to look. Nobody ever gave me a medal for anything, so I don't know what it feels like to be kissed on both cheeks on parade; but the smile of a good scout's approval that he flashed at me was worth more than the stock certificate I bought with my first savings, and by the way subsequently burned as worthless.

Now of course, we have all met folk who say there is nothing in intuition. They will argue about it endlessly; and, funnily enough, they are always the same ones who maintain that an animal has instinct and can't think. Fortunately, in spite of all the modern means for clubbing, coaxing, perverting,and trapping us until we are willing to admit that black is white — or if not that it ought to be — there is still a remnant of the sweet old theory that each of us may have his own opinion without being slandered or imprisoned for it; and it suits my disposition to go down, if I must, with that ship firing all bow guns, I say that intuition is worth more than immediate evidence. I have proved it repeatedly to my own satisfaction, and I don't care a damn what the prophets of all dreary science say.

THERE WAS NOTHING whatever in sight when we reached the end of that rock-pile and lay staring up the bed of the *fiumara*, nothing, I mean, from which a dogmatist could have deduced the neighborhood of danger. If I had wanted to, I might have laughed at Narayan Singh, or have called him to account for robbing me of the sleep I was entitled to.

But my intuition took the form of trusting his, and although a score of birds were going about their normal business, some wild pigs were rooting unconcernedly a hundred yards ahead, and even our friend the panther stopped to lick a paw and look back at us; I was satisfied, without reasoning at all about it, to lie there and watch.

We lay for fifteen or twenty minutes without speaking or moving, while the flies made breakfast off us, and the first reward of patience reached us from the rear. Ayisha could walk like a cat when she chose, but — equally cat and tigresslike — could make plenty of noise when she thought she wasn't watched. A tiger going through the jungle, unless hunting, makes more noise than a buffalo. Knowing that she had escaped from the bivouac unseen, she was taking no further precautions, and we were aware of her clambering over the rock-pile from behind long before she had a chance of seeing us. It was a simple matter then to drop down between boulders and hide ourselves completely.

She followed the left-hand side of the *fiumara*, where most of the rocks were not so difficult to negotiate. She seemed in no hurry, and didn't carry her rifle, which I took for proof that she intended to return to the bivouac after accomplishing her present mission; it seemed likely, too, that she was on her way to meet a friend or she would certainly have brought her weapon.

A little to the front of us on our left hand, on top of the bank of the *fiumara*, stood a dead thorn-tree, so blasted by age and hot wind that very little of it was left except the twisted trunk and one long branch sticking upward at an angle. However, there was another, shorter branch that apparently had fallen a long time ago

Jimgrim, Moses, and Mrs. Aintree

from higher up and got caught in the big one, for it lay nearly parallel along it. I wouldn't have noticed the tree and its branches particularly if Ayisha hadn't glanced up at it more than once, as if she expected to keep her assignation there.

But, seeing she did look up at it with obvious interest, I studied the tree carefully through a crack under the bellies of two boulders. The only peculiarity except its age and withered branches was a filthy old rag, once white, that was tied and twisted to the upper end of the short branch that lay along the other.

And that wasn't so very peculiar. It is customary in that part of the world when a man is buried to tie rags and similar personal souvenirs to the nearest place to which they can be attached. If the dead man was something of a saint, or in other ways important, his grave becomes in course of time a fluttering jumble of odds and ends. Murder being the usual thing, such graves are everywhere; so a soiled rag in a tree wasn't anything to speculate about.

However, Ayisha climbed the bank and went to the tree, but said no prayers, as she probably would have done if keeping tryst with a dead friend. Instead, she illustrated one of the soundest rules of scouting, which is that if you want to signal unobserved, it is better to remove an object that has been standing all along in clear view than to set up a new one. It applies with equal force to hunting. Animals as well as humans are so constituted that they notice new things much more readily than they miss the old.

She didn't wave the rag, but simply laid the branch on the ground and climbed back into the *fiumara*, where she sat down within thirty feet of us, with her back against a rock, so as to be unseen from the direction of our bivouac but visible at once to any one coming toward us down the straight.

I could not see that the signal was answered in any way, but at the end of about five minutes thirty men on camels rounded the bend a furlong in front of us and came straight on, led by a fine looking, slim fellow, whom I presently recognized as the Avenger's brother.

We had only met him once, when Grim checkmated the Avenger in the affair with Ali Higg at Abu Lissan; but he rode with a rather rare alertness and hair-trigger way of glancing to right and left that were unmistakable when considered along with his gorgeously striped cloak and the red and green and gold bands on his head-dress.

He did not pay Ayisha any too much deference, and he and his men made their camels kneel and settled down comfortably in the shade of the high bank before any of them noticed her. Then one of the men called to her to approach; but the Avenger's brother countermanded that, and when he had drunk his fill from one of the goat-skin water-bags he crossed over to where she sat. She remained seated, and he stood throughout the interview.

There was no formal greeting of any kind, and as both of them dropped their voices low it was extremely difficult to catch what was said at a distance of thirty paces. I decided to take the risk of crawling closer, hoping that any sound I might make would be mistaken for that of some small animal. It was easy enough to manage without being seen, because of the way the stones were heaped on one another.

Seeing my intention, Narayan Singh made a gesture with his head in the direction of the bivouac, and started at once to crawl back and waken Grim. It didn't need two of us to listen, but team-work like that calls for something more than heathenism. I have heard Sikhs described as heathens, and have known folk who so describe them, who would have horned in — out of curiosity — to listen, leaving events to take care of themselves.

"I found Jimgrim," I heard Ayisha say, "and he had received the Avenger's message. He was on his way to answer the summons. But he has those thieves with him, and two Indian magicians, and the thieves have magic for Jmil Ras hidden in the camel-loads. If Jmil Ras ever gets that magic there will be no hope for the Avenger."

"Where is Jimgrim?" he demanded after a moment's pause, during which he may or may not have been reviewing with alarm the tribal tales of witchcraft and devilry. I could not see his face.

"He sleeps near by — just down the *fiumara* behind me."

"How many men has he?"

"Nineteen; but he himself is as good as nineteen more," she answered.

"Has he posted men on watch?"

"Two, in good positions, but I think they sleep, for neither of them saw me come away."

"If they are awake can they see in every direction?"

"Yes, except up the *fiumara,* where none would be likely to come because of the rocks. No camel could pass that way, and the men on watch can't see because of the turns."

The Avenger's brother paused again, and through a gap between the rocks I could see him stroke his heard reflectively.

"If I send men to seize those watchmen, they might see my

men first and raise the alarm," he said at last, and I began to hold my breath with that stupid involuntary effort that is first cousin to driving an auto from the rear seat. "So we must leave the camels and go down the *fiumara,*" he continued, pausing again to stroke his beard and think. "They are asleep, eh? We can take our time. Do you think they will fight, if suddenly awakened, or are those thieves likely to surrender at discretion?"

"They will fight!" she answered promptly. "They are the worst firebrands out of El-Kalil."

"*Wallahi!* That is too bad," he exclaimed. "Jimgrim must not be harmed on any account, for he travels under my brother's promise of protection. But nothing was said about those thieves —"

"Who, moreover, seek to carry goods for Jmil Ras — and magic — magic that will turn the mountains into gold and make the Avenger's teeth fall out! You must capture them."

"Nevertheless, if we come on them, and they show fight, and Jimgrim takes the part of his friends, as he has the name of doing, how shall we keep him from harm?" he answered, resuming the stroking of his beard. "*Wallahi!* But this is an awkward business."

"You would do no harm by seizing Jimgrim first," she advised him. "That would not break the law of host and guest for you would have saved his life. He could be set free afterward."

"I wonder what my brother would say to that?"

"He would agree! I know the Avenger."

"Peace, woman! You have only known him a few weeks — I a lifetime. Let me think."

I began to breathe sensibly again, remembering how the Avenger and that man in front of me had spared the life of Ali Higg, their deadliest enemy, at a time when they had him completely in the power. The promise to spare his life had been won by a trick, but they had observed the promise without as much as considering the alternative. The habitual takers of human life and prosecutors of relentless blood-feuds are not by a long shot the worst men in the world.

"Jimgrim must be separated from those thieves," he said at last, "for if not, they will claim his protection, and he ours; whereas, if we get him away from them they can all be in the next world before he knows it. And as for magic — the more of it that Jimgrim can dig out of those loads the better. Let the loads be his, if he claims them, but those thieves have cumbered the earth too long already. Go you back, woman. Waken Jimgrim quietly, and persuade him to return with you to this place, saying that one man waits to speak with him alone. Bring him along the high ground, and my men will use the *fiumara*."

"But what if he brings two or three?"

"No matter. I will keep a handful here to deal with any body-guard he brings. While Jimgrim is kept talking here my men will attend to the other matter. It is time the crows were given a good meal!"

She argued a little yet. I don't think she relished her job much, or that she was any too sure of luring Grim into the trap. But he cut short her arguments abruptly with a string of sulfurous oaths and turned his back on her to go and instruct his men.

So she began rather slowly and reluctantly to climb back over the tumbled rocks. And as soon as her back was toward me I began very cautiously to follow her, thankful that she went so slowly, because I had the double task of keeping hidden from both front and rear. I was minded to have a talk with her before either of us reached Grim's tent, but not so soon that she should be able to shout an alarm to the Avenger's brother.

So we made one turn and the half of another before I called a halt. There was an enormous round boulder in the middle of the *fiumara* bed at that point, and she was just about to feel her way around it, stepping gingerly from rock to rock, when I called out.

"*Ya sit* Ayisha!" ["O lady Ayisha."]

She stopped as if shot, saw me, and made an instinctive dive into her clothes for a weapon. But all she had was a dagger — not the one that I had taken from her and tossed to Narayan Singh, but a Persian thing with a curved blade. She drew it and showed her teeth pretty much as our friend the panther ha behaved an hour before.

It was pretty to watch the changing emotions on her face as I drew nearer. Her first instinctive intention to kill me if she could gave place to realization of the hopelessness, as well as the useless-ness of that; next to almost hysterical despair; and then to cun-ning, and a flashing smile as sweet as sunshine on the morning dew. Lord! But she was pretty when she beamed at you that way.

However, I kept both eyes on her and trusted to luck for my footing, for she might have thrown that dagger, and I've seen her throw one mighty straight, as I hope to tell one of these days.

"*Mashallah!* Why this secrecy?" she said with a laugh as soon as I drew close. But she kept the dagger in her hand, and if she had been anything other than a woman I would have drawn my pistol.

Wisdom and self-respect don't always seem to run in double harness, do they?

"I knew all along that you were there listening," she said mockingly. "You made more noise than a frightened horse!"

I knew that wasn't true, but decided to test it all the same.

"You might have seen me coming out of the tent," said I, "for it was difficult to hide just then; but after that I thought I followed pretty well."

"Your magic didn't work, O *Miyan!* I looked back and saw you four times between the tents and that tree, and I could hear you coming behind me all the way."

Well, that was just like a woman. I can't imagine why she chose to lie about it, unless to reduce my conceit and make me more amenable to argument.

"No matter," I answered. "I heard what you said to the Avenger's brother, and what he said to you. That is the main point."

At that she lied again, remarkably readily. I'm not blaming her any more than Grim did at any time. I like the wench, and dare say she will go far under the new régime just dawning in Arab lands. But she had learned political ambition with no more leaven of redeeming altruism than Grim had been able to teach her in less than a dozen days. Moreover, she had had time, and lots of opportunity to forget the lesson learned from him; so now, caught in a predicament, she lied as her ancestresses always did.

"You must not make trouble between me and Jimgrim," she said, pleading — but keeping the dagger in full view still. "You are a *Miyan* and do not understand. There was a plot to capture Jimgrim, and to render him helpless by killing all his men, so that he would have to obey the Avenger whether he will or not. But I love Jimgrim. I am on his side. *Wallahi!* I would die for his sake. Therefore I pretended to agree to the plot, and came to meet Jimgrim in the desert. Then, this morning, I kept the tryst here to make sure of everything, for fear of losing Jimgrim's confidence by giving him a false alarm. And now I go to warn him."

"*Bismillah!* He ought to be grateful to you!" said I.

"You think so?"

"Why not? But for you the trap might have been set far more effectually. Let us go now and wake the weasel from his sleep lest the rabbits catch him."

"Are you sneering at me, *Miyan*? Have a care!"

"Who would sneer at such a beautiful princess?" I answered.

"By the whiskers of the Prophet, it was your cleverness that shed light in a dark place. Come along, let us find Jimgrim."

But she stood at bay still, with her back against the bulge of the great boulder, and I think she would have stuck her dagger into me if the footing had been better, and I less alert.

"Are you and I enemies or friends?" she demanded.

"All Jimgrim's friends are mine," said I.

"I suspect you," she answered. "I think you are like an adder lying in the sand that bites the camels' heels. You are one of those who speak fair and act foul."

Nothing like seeing yourself as a woman sees you, is there! But I'm better at self-defense with fists than tongue, and rather irreverently prone to laugh at criticism.

"I don't think you need feel afraid of me," I said; and she tossed up her chin as if she were the Queen of Sheba putting one of King Solomon's court attendants in his place.

"Afraid of you? It is you who should fear me, *Miyan!* I am well able to care for myself, but you are —"

"I have the name of a magician," I interrupted.

But one of the strangest things in the world is that people who believe in black magic and witchcraft also believe that they can overawe the magician or the witch, much as if a prizefighter with gloves on should threaten a man in an armored aeroplane.

"Use your magic the way I bid you, then, or you shall suffer for it!" she retorted. "Use it to protect Jimgrim now without setting him against me!"

"So be it, O lady Ayisha," I answered; and I began to make passes with my hands, and to quote about all the Latin I remember from my school-days.

"*Quadrupedante putrem sonitu quatit ungula campum!*" I remarked by way of final emphasis; and there is a sort of galloping thump to that line when you say it properly that commands respect. She was distinctly a shade paler by the time I was through.

"Go along ahead of me now," I said, "and judge for yourself whether the spell has worked or not. And afterward, if you are satisfied, you must give me credit for obliging you."

So she went ahead, full of mingled pride, superstitious fear, and curiosity; and I chuckled in her wake, for I was sure of three things — that Narayan Singh had wakened Grim long ago; that Grim had already made arrangements for the protection of Ali Baba and his men; and that Grim was the last man who would "set himself" or be set against Ayisha for any consideration. He isn't given to petty personalities, or to complaining of his tools, but plays up to the best instincts of friend and enemy alike.

But I never suspected how perfectly he had turned the trick for me, nor what prodigious respect Ayisha would have for my magic as the result. Having lost time talking, she hurried down the *fiumara*, leaping like a doe from rock to rock, and I had a hard time keeping pace. In fact, I failed to do it, and she turned the last corner more than fifty yards ahead of me. There she stopped dead, and when I overtook her she stared at me open-mouthed, saying nothing for about a minute.

Grim was gone. So were the tents. So were the camels. So were Ali Baba and his men, and Narayan Singh. There wasn't a trace or a sound of them, and except for a few deep scratches in the sand you could hardly tell there had been a bivouac pitched there.

I don't approve of too much crowing over a victory, especially when nine-tenths of it is due to another man's quick wit; but I couldn't resist the impulse then.

"Does the spell seem to have worked, princess?" I asked triumphantly.

"*Miyan*, you are a great magician!" she answered. "You must obey me now in all things, and we will send Jmil Ras to Jehannum. After that I will be a great queen!"

Chapter IX

"Ask the camel of Jmil Ras!"

WELL, THAT WAS a fine plan of Ayisha's; but as Grim must have done a heap of swift guesswork and would likely be grateful for hard facts, my first business was to find him. I thought it probable he would hide somewhere and wait for me before deciding on his gambit; but what he actually had done was to stow the men and camels in a hollow about three hundred yards to the left as you stood facing up the *fiumara,* with Narayan Singh on guard to keep them in there, and to come back himself in search of me.

He peered down over the bank from between two rocks just as I was starting off to look for him in the opposite direction — having guessed wrongly that he would follow along old camel-prints in order to gain time by making his pursuers stop and think.

"Are you running away with Ayisha?" he called down. "Ayisha, I'm surprised; I thought that you and I were friends!"

"Does he seem set against you yet?" I asked her, and she almost purred at me like a fed cat.

We climbed up the bank, and in a hurry I told Grim all I knew of the Avenger's brother's plan, giving Ayisha's version of her connection with it because she was listening and checking me up. But I contrived to wink at him without her seeing, and Ayisha was the only person fooled.

I like to watch Grim make his mind up when he has all the facts. It reminds you of the breech-bolt action of a quick-firing gun that one moment is all wide open waiting for a charge, and the next shuts tight with a click and is ready for instant business. You can almost hear the click. The expression of his face changes very little, and he says less; but you know that a deal has been closed, so to speak, and that nothing remains to do but follow him to the conclusion.

"Coming down the *fiumara*, eh?"

He cast his eyes swiftly over the landscape, and the general drift of that thought was easy to understand. As I explained, whoever used the *fiumara* for a road would have to leave it where the boulder-cluttered figure **S** began and make a detour, which was really a short cut. You could see where hundreds of men had done that very thing; and as humans are like cattle in following the line of least exertion, the track had come to look almost like a road, leading in a wide semicircle along the lowest level. The head of a man on camel-back would hardly have been visible at any point along it to any one peering over the rim of the *fiumara*.

"Come on!" said Grim, and led the way to the hollow where the men all waited.

Then he sent Narayan Singh on foot to hide himself on top of the bank where the figure **S** curved toward us, with orders to signal the movements of the men below. He was to raise his left fist once for each man he could see, and his right fist to mean that they were coming forward. If he raised his rifle that would mean that something unforeseen was happening, in which case Grim would send a messenger to him to learn particulars.

We waited for Narayan Singh to take up position, old Ali Baba fuming impatiently because Grim wouldn't order a retreat.

"By Allah, Jimgrim, hasn't the Sikh told you that those are the Avenger's men? They will cut my sons' throats and steal this merchandise as quick as look at it! We have good camels, man; let us run, and come at Jmil Ras by another way. I have my bargain to keep!"

"You made a bargain to obey me!" Grim answered, and the old man left off talking. His sons and grandsons were as full of fear as he, but perfectly content to fulfill any terms their sire had committed them to. They were tough, and no observers of any commandments that the West pays lip-service to, except the Fifth, and if their days are not long in the land in consequence some sort of explanation should be due them from the missionaries.

Narayan Singh shot up his left fist twenty-nine times, and Grim led forward. Our destination was the blasted tree from which Ayisha had made her signal, although the track we followed re-entered the *fiumara* at a point considerably beyond that. We brought all the baggage beasts along — went forward, in fact, as if just arriving on the scene after a long march, and I rode beside

Grim giving him an exact description of the *fiumara* where the Avenger's brother waited.

Even so, it wasn't quite obvious what he intended to do, although he seemed in no doubt whatever. Narayan Singh's right fist kept shooting up in token that our would-be murderers were holding their course steadily. They were no doubt going slowly so as to make no noise, surprize being the main element of their strategy; so we went slowly too, in order to have them as far away from us as possible by the time we reached the tree.

As we held the shorter course and were mounted, we went at least two to their one, so that by the time we reached our goal they were about half-way to theirs, well out of call of the Avenger's brother, but not far enough along to discover our ruse and return or start hue and cry, which was about the ideal arrangement.

Grim ordered us to dismount fifty yards to the left of the blasted tree and hobble the camels. Then, leaving Ayisha in charge of Mujrim as a precaution against her giving the alarm too soon, he walked to the tree along with me and Ali Baba, and stood still and silent for nearly a minute, smiling as he watched the men who waited patiently below.

We were three to three; or so it must have seemed to the Avenger's brother when he looked up. He didn't seem surprized at first, for he expected Grim; and I daresay he thought Ayisha had stayed behind to direct the plunder of our bivouac, which would be about the normal behavior of a princess of that land. Nearly all tribal battles end in the plunder of one camp or the other by the women-folk, whose principal value to their husbands is their ability to garner wealth while the men gather martial laurels and notch their rifle-butts.

He rose and bowed to Grim, smiling handsomely — a regular Paladin making his guest free of all the desert.

"Greeting, Jimgrim! God give your honor long life! May the blessing of the Most High bring you peace and prosperity! My brother sent me to bid you welcome."

"Greeting!" Grim called down. And then, like the man who met Jehu son of Nimshi in the Bible story — "Is it peace?"

"Peace between us, Jimgrim! Come down here and rest a while."

"Three men," Grim answered, "and more than thirty camels? You speak of peace. Is this an ambush or a trap?"

"Allah do more to me, if I would lay a hand on you, Jimgrim! There is a party of miscreants near here, whom my men have gone to settle an account with. As soon as they have attended to that business we will start for Abu Kem, if your honor pleases."

The Avenger's brother was looking very hard indeed at Ali Baba, whose face was more than half hidden in the folds of his loose head-dress. He had only seen the old man once before, but seemed to think he recognized him nevertheless. Grim whispered to me without moving his lips much, and I stepped back a few paces to make a sign to our men.

"Perhaps you need help to deal with those miscreants?" Grim suggested. "One friend should help another, and where there are miscreants there is no peace. I pray you, let me lend a hand."

"Nay! Your honor's life is too important to be risked in such a little matter. Rather come down into the *fiumara,* and —"

The smile left the face of the Avenger's brother suddenly. But he acted well. He kept his chin high, and his gaze at Grim did not falter for a second. Our men, stepping forward all in line, had reached the *fiumara*'s edge, and stood staring solemnly down at the three and the camels. Their rifles were cocked, but that is as normal in the desert as the old-time pirate custom of firing a shotted salute to another pirate ship.

There was no more than a hint yet, although a broad one, of reprisals in kind, but the Avenger's brother and his two men were nervous, and kept their hands off their own weapons with an obvious effort. They were absolutely at Grim's mercy, camels and all, but Grim offered no explanation, not even suggesting by a smile or gesture what the outcome was to be.

Grim is past master at that game of keeping silent until the other man commits himself; he plays his tune on the strings of human character, choosing carefully; for, as I have heard him say, there is always one string you can tune the others by. It was the Avenger's brother's turn to speak, and almost anything he might say — he being a chivalrous and honorable man according to his lights — was going to be a chord that Grim could use; and as a matter of fact he plucked the simplest string of all.

"Is it peace?" he asked, using Grim's formula.

"That is for you to say," Grim answered, looking rather stern, and wholly noncommittal. "It seems to me, I find you unprotected."

"True. I claim your protection, Jimgrim!"

Grim saluted him in the graceful, lordly desert fashion, head bent and hand to forehead.

"These are my men," he answered. "Their goods are my

goods; their weapons my weapons; their honor my honor. Let it be their honor to protect both thee and me."

Ali Baba is a wise old fox, quicker than most professional thieves to understand fine points of honor, and totally different from the Western sharp, in that he will observe the fine point, once agreed on, to the death. He is no slick-tongued shyster, pinning down a victim to rules that he himself won't observe, although he is slick and slippery as well as an outrageous liar when it suits him.

He made an instant signal down the line and held up his right hand in token of agreement to the bargain; every one of his sons and grandsons — except Mujrim, who was still keeping Ayisha out of sight — followed suit. They swore aloud then in the name of Allah that the Avenger's brother's life was in their keeping; and at a sign from Grim, Mujrim, leading Ayisha by the hand, came forward and did the same. thing.

"Jimgrim, thou art a prince of tricksters!" said Ali Baba, grinning sidewise at him with his old face screwed into a thousand wrinkles. "But have a care! One trick begets another!"

Under the unwritten desert law it would now be the unspeakable offense for either side to do the other an injury; but you can drive a coach and four horses between the provisions of any law that ever was made, unless there is means of enforcing it, and the greatest sticklers for law and etiquette are invariably splitters of fine hairs. It would have stretched imagination too far to pretend that we were absolutely safe now, but we were safer than we had been.

Ayisha was the weakest point remaining at the moment. She followed Grim down into the *fiumara*, and the black look flashed sidewise at her by the Avenger's brother was no good sign; reasonably and rightly he regarded her as the cause of his predicament, and if she had not purposely betrayed him there was no way of his knowing that, nor much likelihood of his believing it.

But Grim didn't propose to waste time over domestic squabbles just then. The men who had been sent to murder our crew were likely to draw blank any minute and come hurrying back, and although they would probably obey the Avenger's brother, if he should have time to forbid their attacking us, that wasn't much more than probable; they would see us between them and their camels — appraise the odds at three to two in their favor — and just as likely as not open fire on us from the cover of the jumbled *fiumara* rocks.

If they should return along the high ground, on the other hand, they might snap up Narayan Singh on the way and then pounce on our beasts with their valuable loads; and if there is one safe bet in the world it is this — that when plunder has once fallen into Arab hands it needs more than the orders of their Sheikh to make them give it up again.

SO GRIM SENT ONE MAN running for Narayan Singh, and ordered all our camels brought down into the *fiumara*. They came tumbling down like a lot of double-ended dummies, some of the loaded ones falling and rolling, and all roaring their fear of the goat-path loud enough to set the *fiumara* echoing and warn whomever it might interest a mile away.

But you can't be discourteous to a man like the Avenger's brother — not, that is to say, if you are wise and have a bargain with him that is based on desert etiquette, and whatever his secret impatience Grim spoke as courteously as they say the Spanish torturers used to in the days when one gentleman would invite another to be seated on the iron chair before the glowing coals.

"If your honor would be kind enough to agree, I would like to take all my men and all your honor's camels about a mile farther up the *fiumara*."

"In the name of the Prophet, why?"

"In order to wait there for your honor's men."

"But my men will expect to find me here!"

"*Inshallah*, we shall disappoint them. By your honor's favor we will leave one man here to explain the circumstances to them. Otherwise, if they should come on us suddenly in this place there might be an accident."

"*Mashallah!*" the Avenger's brother retorted hotly. "You doubt my good faith?"

"Allah forbid! But since our mutual honor is involved, my good faith obliges me to protect yours. Let there be no chance for misunderstanding between your men and mine."

The Avenger's brother did not like it, but couldn't refuse a command put so politely. He had the good taste to beg Grim's pardon for not having thought of the plan first, and they spent at least two minutes paying each other compliments, while Ali Baba fumed inwardly, but stood still with a magnificently assumed air of patience.

The old fox, too, had manners, and although technically the Avenger's brother was in no position to refuse any demand whatever, he waited for their owner's personal permission before laying hand on the camels or letting his sons take a step toward them.

So all the conventions were observed, and it was the Avenger's brother, not Grim, who at last requested Ali Baba to take all the men and beasts and to honor the universe by casting his noble shadow on it about a mile farther up the *fiumara*.

Ali Baba answered at once that the Avenger's brother's lightest wish was a command to him, second only in importance to the law of Allah; and, taking one thing with another, I don't believe two Western nations at daggers drawn could have saved each other's faces more gracefully.

One of the two men who had stayed with the Avenger's brother to welcome Grim was left behind to greet the returning men and take the sting out of their disappointment, and away the rest of us went to look for a better place in which to await them and, if necessary, defend ourselves against attack; for, having made no agreement with Grim or any one else, they might elect to solve the problem in their own way by rescuing their master.

As things turned out we never discovered what course they would have taken, for circumstances played into Grim's hands in such fashion that all the Avenger's brothers' men became our debtors within the hour — circumstances and Jmil Ras. And we were to learn more about Jmil Ras before the unexpected happened.

Not much was said as we trailed up the *fiumara*, Grim and Ali Baba side by side with the Avenger's brother bringing up the rear. But Ayisha ranged alongside me, and was by no means dumb.

"Now for thy magic, *Miyan!*" she commanded. "Thus far it has worked well and Jimgrim hasn't quarreled with me; in which he shows wisdom, for I am his friend. But that Achmet Saoud, the Avenger's brother, looked blackly at me. You must poison him. The son of sixty dogs suspected me of plotting with Ibrahim ben Ali, but could prove nothing. Now he will add that to this and make a mountain of it.

"He and the Avenger are not like ordinary brothers, for they do not hate each other, and what the one says the other agrees to; so there is trouble in store for me in Abu Kem unless you poison him. You say that magic stuff of yours will make the teeth fall out? Good. Do that for a beginning! I wish to see it work. Then, while he bewails his lost teeth, you may kill him altogether in some other way."

I think I have said at least a dozen times that I am no diplomatist, my forte being patience and direct action; but it seemed best to me just then to divide the honors with Narayan Singh, who, excepting those rather rare intervals when bazaar whisky stirs bats in his belfry, is a master of Machiavellian finesse.

"I must confess to you that there are two of us magicians. I can't work without consulting the Pathan," said I, "nor he without consulting me. And you've made it difficult for me to cast spells for you by mocking the Pathan when he makes love to you, so that he is angry and will agree to nothing."

Don't you think that was passing the buck pretty smartly on the spur of the moment? I mean, for a man who hasn't ever fooled himself that he was quick-witted. It convinced Ayisha by a process of inference not only that my magic powers were really so, but also that I should be treated more respectfully; for, where one magician might be dirked for disobedience, two, working in partnership would have to be managed gingerly.

"But his love is foolish," she protested. "I wouldn't be the wife of such a man if there were no men left! He makes himself ridiculous and me a scandal!"

Then, with a subtle sidewise smile at me and a lift of her arched eyebrows — "What a pity that the wrong magician vows he loves me!"

Well, there you are. You see, a man can't pit his brains successfully against a woman's, and you've got to use brute force, or run away, or else be defeated in the end. Grim is the only exception to that rule whom I have met, and I wouldn't bet on Grim too far, if a woman once got half a real chance at him.

If mine was a quick-fire diplomatic shot, hers was twice as quick and twenty times as cunning. Having no intention in the world of yielding herself to any Indian — a race she openly despised — she proposed to flirt with both of us and play one off against the other. You may say I could refuse; that I might have claimed the prerogative of a *darwaish,* who is supposed to have turned his back on the delights of this world, flirting the very first among them.

But unless I should walk to some extent into her net, I would be depriving Grim of half my usefulness. He was counting on me for inside information, which only Ayisha could provide. So the only practicable opening she had left me was a mighty mean one, and I tried that, *faute de mieux.*

"If that Pathan were to catch me looking at you covetously, he would knife me in the back at the first chance," I answered lamely.

She laughed delightedly at that. Nothing could have pleased her more than the notion of two magicians fighting to possess her, with the ultimate refusal hers in any case.

"I have seen you fight," she answered. "You fought Mujrim, who is twice as strong as the Pathan; and I know your magic can protect you for, you remember, I stuck my dagger into you and it only grazed your leg."

"That Pathan has killed a score of men in Palestine," I answered, "and Allah knows how many more before he came here."

"Twenty men to his hand? Good. Kill him then, and cut one-and-twenty notches on your rifle-butt!"

"I have to consider Jimgrim, who employs us both," I answered, "and Jimgrim is considering Jmil Ras. Tell me about Jmil Ras. He is called a very great magician. If that is true, I mustn't kill the Pathan, because it will take the two of us to overcome him. Tell me all you know about him."

"Nobody knows anything about him, except that he is handsome and in league with the Devil! Some say this, and some say that. He can make the dead men talk in their graves."

"How do you know that?"

"Because he said there was gold in the mountain and began to dig for it. But there were graves of saints there, and the people said he should not desecrate the sacred ground. So he cast a spell, and each of the saints began to talk out of his tomb, commanding him to dig the gold out in order that they might have peace.

"The saints said that if the gold were once taken the devils would go away forever, having nothing left to stay there for. A hundred men who were present heard them say it, and the voice of each saint was different from the other, some speaking faintly, as if from far off, and others very loud, as if close at hand; but they all said the same thing, although some of them used different words."

"That sounds like strong magic," said I. "What else does he do?"

"Sometimes men begin to doubt him, because the *mallims*, who did not hear the saints speak, come and say that it is sacrilege to dig wherever saints' tombs are. Then he does unbelievable things, turning bullets into money, gathering gold pieces from the air, discovering this and that thing in the clothing of men who never saw the things before. Moreover, he can make a camel talk; when it opens its mouth words like a man's come forth, so that nowadays folk have a saying that you should ask the camel of Jmil Ras."

"Who was his father?" I demanded, thinking that might lead to revelations.

"The father of insolence and cunning and all unexpectedness!" she answered. "None can foretell his next move or explain his last one; yet he foretells everything. Whenever men gather to attack him, he seems aware of it and makes the first attack, sometimes by night, dispersing the first-comers before they are reinforced, so that now men are unwilling to gather against him, saying that none can fight against the powers of darkness."

We reached a bend in the *fiumara* where it would be possible for twenty men to render a good account of themselves against thirty, and I had just finished repeating that conversation word for word to Grim when a lot of intermittent, ragged firing broke out somewhere about a mile behind us in the direction from which we had come. Rifles always seem to me to have voices that express emotions in their own field as distinctly as those of men and animals; it's one of those things you can't explain, that nevertheless convince you after years of more or less promiscuous campaigning.

You can't persuade me that the sound made, for instance, by a lost man firing to attract attention to himself is the same as that made by a hunter shooting game, and I am not alone in my conviction. Grim, for one, agrees with me, and so do most desert Arabs I have talked with.

That was desperate firing, done by men fighting for their lives, alternately taking careful aim and then blazing away furiously in a moment's panic. Grim got out his glasses, and leaving the camels in the *fiumara* the whole lot of us followed him to the top of a sandy hillock that provided a good view of the countryside for miles.

We could all see what was happening, but Grim with the glasses was the only one who could make out details. The Avenger's brother's men — invisible among the stones in the bed of the *fiumara* — were being attacked by more than a hundred, who had arrived unseen from the eastward — for their camels were hobbled in a group on the east bank — and were now firing into the *fiumara* from both sides. It looked like a merciless effort at extermination; but having had experience of those jumbled boulders I was willing to bet that it couldn't succeed unless the men on top were willing to go down and finish the business hand to hand.

Ali Baba was the first to speak, and he was all for flight, as usual. That was the fox instinct.

"*Wallahi!* Jimgrim, why wait! This whole business is a trap to get those goods of mine! Those are the Avenger's men attacking, and they think it is we who are down in the *fiumara!* This Avenger's brother is a treacherous fellow sent to block this end of the trap while the others attacked from the rear. Trust me! I see through the whole plot! Now be wise, Jimgrim! Listen to an old man, who has come alive, thanks to Allah, out of a thousand tight places! Jmil Ras is the man to depend on; ride as the wind goes, then, for Jmil Ras!"

"What does Jmil Ras look like?" Grim asked casually.

"In the name of Allah! Who cares what he looks like?"

"Black mustache? No beard or whiskers? Does he wear a cock's plume stuck in his head-dress?"

"Yes!" said Ayisha. "He makes magic with it!"

Grim returned the glasses to their case, and smiled at me.

"We've found your friend Jeremy," he said. "D'you think he'd recognize you?"

"Not in this disguise, I'll bet he wouldn't."

"Can you think of any way of making him recognize you? He's out for trouble by the look of things, and there'll be a mess if he divides his force and sends fifty or so to tackle us while he deals with that bunch in the *fiumara.* Think now!"

I'm not pretending to explain how thoughts come in a crisis. I only know that if they didn't there'd be precious few of us alive to carry on this world's affairs.

"Yes," I said, "if I can get within a hundred yards of him, and if that's Jeremy, I can call the fighting off and we'll issue rain checks."

"Good!" he answered. "Go and try."

I tell you, I like that fellow Grim. He knows how to pick a man for a certain task, and then turn him loose without both ears chock-full of limiting instructions. He turned and drove our party back under cover without another word to me.

Chapter X

"You're a fallen angel, Ramsden!"

I TOOK MY RIFLE, not that I proposed to use it, but for old acquaintance sake, because all my stalking has been after big game and, say what you like, we humans are creatures of habit just as much as the animals we hunt. I once knew a man who couldn't find his way in the city without an umbrella, and I was one of the very few who never laughed at him.

It wasn't easy stalking. For one thing I had to go fast unless those men among the boulders were to be decimated; for another it was practically open country, with only that sandy ridge running nearly parallel to the *fiumara* to take advantage of. But, as probably a million men discovered in the great war, you can hide behind a pebble when the other fellow isn't looking for you and inside a few square feet of shadow even when he is. A brown Bedouin cloak is hot and in your way when you're using hands and knees, but even in strong sunlight shades away into the desert color-scheme beyond belief.

It was nervous work, though, for I knew that two score eyes and a pair of Zeiss binoculars were watching me from under cover in the rear, and there wasn't one of them likely to miss a fine point. True, I wasn't going to get written up in the papers, and read an account next day of how badly I had bungled the fourth hole; and Grim wasn't going to pass remarks whatever happened; but I function best out of the public eye, and would never have made a good gladiator or anything like that, although I enjoy using what faculties I have so thoroughly that old women of both sexes have called me an instinctive savage.

I think I made the distance — say a mile along the straight

from where Grim watched to the boulder I had singled out to work magic from — in a minute or two under half an hour, and I daresay each five minutes of that time cost the life of a man, although I've lost no sleep over it. I didn't start the fight, and I didn't hesitate to save time by taking chances across the open when a circuit would have cost ten more minutes.

Anyhow, unseen as far as I know, I reached the cover of a boulder shaped something like a dog's head, rather more than a hundred yards to the rear of the firing-line, and wondered what to do next, for there was so much din of battle going on — shooting and yelling and running to and fro for a better pot-shot at somebody among the stones below — that you couldn't have made yourself heard at that distance with a fog-horn.

Every minute or so somebody would yell, and jump up, and dance delightedly, swearing he had shot a man, grabbing his mates here and there to brag to them and explain in pantomime exactly where the bullet hit, and how the victim fell over; but fortunately you can't always believe an Arab's account of casualties any more than what you read at home in the daily paper. But I saw three men drilled cleanly through the head as they leaned over the edge of the fiumara, so it wasn't any child's play that was going on, and the men in the trap weren't selling their lives cheap.

I could see the man who Grim had said was Jmil Ras, but it was several minutes before he turned enough toward me for me to make sure he was really Jeremy. He had a black cock's feather stuck in the camel's-hair band that bound his Arab head-dress, and that was unusual enough to mark him for no ordinary native of the country; but it might have meant that he had shot an Australian in the war and chose that way of boasting of the feat. Some men's rifle-butts have so many notches cut in them that they invent new ways of signifying that their foes are dead.

But when he turned my way there wasn't a doubt of him. He had lost a little of his youthful look, but he was Jeremy Ross if twelve o'clock is noon.

He wasn't encouraging his men or giving any orders, but gave the impression of letting them have their fling. I saw him laugh aloud when one of his own fire-breathing fanatics was shot dead in the act of boasting, but on the other hand he dragged the wounded from the firing-line with his own hands and stowed them under cover behind rocks.

In fact, it was the strangest picnic, and he the strangest host I had ever watched, and how to call his attention without drawing the fire of twenty rifles on myself seemed an unsolvable mystery.

But I was there to make magic, and seeing I had to take a chance of some sort I decided that if my nerves weren't quite as steady, perhaps, as Jeremy's at the moment, my life was at least as sweet as his; and if his nerves were really the steadier, then a close shave wouldn't hurt him. He sat down on a rock and began unscrewing the stopper of a service flask, and I know I hoped the rock he sat on was as hot as the infernal thing I had to sprawl across. It is rarely that two men shoot their best in exactly the same position; I like to rest my belly and elbow over a solid support of some kind.

The risk was that I might drill a bullet through his head when he lifted the flask to drink, but that seemed better than being shot before I could get word with him; so I held my breath and took aim six inches to the left of his mouth, and let drive as he lifted the thing across the foresight.

If I weren't a good shot I should be one of the unteachables who belong in the orderly places where you buy your meat in shops and don't cross the street until the cop gives you permission; for Lord knows I have had experience enough.

And as luck would have it, Jeremy held the flask by the neck, so that there was a good hand's breadth of brown felt cover between my eye and the sky-line; the bullet went plump through the middle of that, sploshing the water into his face, knocking the flask galley-west, and spoiling his drink abominably, but doing no other damage.

And of course he glanced in my direction, although I never heard tell what human sense it is that tells a man which way a bullet came. I'm willing to swear he couldn't have heard the report of my rifle, because of the din made by his own rapscallions. I could see his lips move as he swore, but it wouldn't have been Jeremy if he hadn't laughed at the same time; and he wouldn't have been human if he hadn't reached for his rifle, but before he could touch it I gave tongue.

"*Coo-eee-eee!*"

Lord! How he jumped and stared; and the look of delight, that flashed across his face was worth twice that dusty crawl to come and see. He couldn't have heard that long Australian yell for more than two years, and it took all the sudden fight out of him. He let the rifle lie, and stood up — a fair mark for any one inclined to murder him — and putting both hands to his mouth yelled back:

"Coo-eee-eee! Coo-eee-eee!"

Now that was genuine magic. There was no hocus-pocus, superstition or mechanical ingenuity in any way connected with it. I had made a sound that touched the inner heart-strings of a fellow man and switched his whole attention instantly from the absorbing business of a fight to me — alone — a bearded, brown, presumptive Indian on a hot rock. He turned his back entirely on the screaming fighting men, *coo-ee-ed* again between his hands, and came running toward me with the awkward half-galloping gait of a horseman in a hurry.

You may say what you like about Free Masonry, and I say nothing, being wise in that respect. But when you're in a tight place in foreign parts and yearn for action without argument, just yell *"Coo-eee!"* to a Cornstalk; and if all the Devil and his accomplices are boiling between him and you, you'll see Hell shifted and its legions made afraid, because there isn't any inferno, and never was, that can douse an Australian's chivalry.

It's a new chivalry, because theirs is a new land; but there's more of the old in it than you dare try to explain to an Australian, unless you want to swap punches. They don't like being told that England with long-bow and leather jacket taught them anything. The point to bear in mind is, that in a tight place, in any circumstances, *"Coo-eee"* works. And now that I've spilled the beans, I'll leave Australians to sweep them up again, and get on with the story.

I guess he thought I was an Indian until he came within ten yards of me, and Australians all draw the color-line tight and hard, don't forget that. But I once saw an Australian sluice himself from head to foot and go through burning grass to rescue an Afghan, simply because the Afghan had once driven camels across the desert in West Aus.

When he came close enough I grinned, and called out:

"Hello Jeremy! Who'd have thought of meeting you again? What's your difficulty this time?"

"Oh, you, is it?" he answered. "Well, I'll be damned! Where did you get those whiskers? Say; that fellow Grim turned out a dandy — perfect Jim-pippin of a man! What became of him?"

We shook hands as if we were pumping water, and he sat down there on the rock beside me, with all that fighting going on, and began to talk as if we had seen each other yesterday.

"Hah-hah! Too bad I couldn't kidnap Grim along with me. He and I'd have added Arabia to the Commonwealth! Hah! What happened to him? I heard tales of him using this part for a checkerboard, shoving the Sheikhs from square to square as he pleased."

"He's close by," I said. "He sent me to tell you to call this fighting off."

"The Hell he did! Same old Grim, eh? He'd hand out orders to the Almighty and watch him do it! But listen a minute: I came out to meet a man named Ali Baba, who's supposed to he bringing me dynamite and jam. I'd walk to Jericho to get some jam. These parts aren't healthy for a hilly-and-bluey column on the march, so I got the idea to round 'em up and kind o' nurse 'em, see? Came out with a hundred men — best gang of Bible-minded robbers ever you set eyes on — and sent out a scouting party of twenty at dawn to look for my supply column.

"They looked about and didn't see much, so they cooked it up between 'em to rest in this *fiumara*, where I couldn't see 'em loafing from the skyline, knowing I'd twist their tails to beat the Queen if I caught 'em at it. And while they parked their hams down there along come thirty sons-of-guns and go for 'em without notice! Shot nine men before you could say Christmas, and waded in to chew hash out of the rest!

"I know who they are; they belong to that Willy-boy who calls himself the Avenger, and he's got it in for me. I haven't treated him strict enough — too soft-hearted by a darned sight — been teaching him kindergarten — stripped his men and sent 'em back to him naked and that kind of thing, whereas what he needs is strafing by a Hun.

"Top o' that my men were sore all the way through at being jumped on that way, and I don't blame 'em. They swore by Allah and the Prophet to wipe that outfit off the map, and I turned 'em loose to do it. Call 'em off, eh? Might as well try to whistle dingoes off a sick sheep! They mean to clean up, bones and all."

"They have my sympathy," said I, "but it don't suit Grim's book, Jeremy old man. He puts it this way — he'd regard it as a special favor if you'd call this game off, because he's got a hotter one waiting to begin, and all this noise you're making spoils his aim."

"Does he know I'm here?"

"You bet."

"And he asks it as a favor?"

"Certainly."

"Well I'll be damned! If Grim's not a good sport, there isn't one! Don't he think I'm a deserter?"

"He didn't say."

"Well, he's the boy for me! Let's see if we can't oblige him. Stay there."

He ran off, skipping and jumping, toward the firing-line without another word and, seeming to pick them carefully, dragged back two men by the scruff of the neck and shook them until they paid attention to him.

I suppose I ought to have stayed where I was, because there isn't any sense in walking about among flying bullets unless you have to, and Grim was counting on me for information and support later on. But women aren't the only people who are curious, and anyhow I went.

The only men down in the *fiumara* who were visible had been dead some while, and it was doubtful whether you could bury them without a rake, because Jeremy's crowd on both banks were wasting ammunition riddling the corpses full of holes. And I suppose each man would notch his rifle after each shot! But those who were still keeping up a hot fire from under cover must have been getting short of ammunition, and it didn't call for much shrewdness to figure out that they would surrender if given the chance.

I don't know what Jeremy said to the two men he had singled out. Maybe he threatened them with black magic or something of that sort, but whatever it was it took effect. He sent one man to cross the *fiumara* below the bend and spread the order from mouth to mouth on the far side, and after about ten minutes the firing ceased. Then Jeremy himself stood as close to the edge of the *fiumara* as he dared and offered quarter in the name of Allah, saying that any one who cared to claim protection now might have it.

There were only eleven men left alive, and several of those were seriously wounded, but they had enough presence of mind left not to show themselves as long as Jeremy's men were in evidence.

When he called his men off, and one spirit more daring than the rest had crawled out to take a look, the remainder emerged one by one like rabbits out of holes, whereat Jeremy told them to bury their dead and look sharp about it.

That reassured them, especially when a couple of rough hoes were tossed down for the purpose, it being a Moslem's principal obsession to be buried when he dies, just as a Hindu wants to have his body burned. But the job was perfunctory; they buried the totally dead ones first under about a foot of sand, with a few stones piled on top to make the hyenas work for a meal — and then dug rather deeper graves for the men who should have been dead, even if they weren't, and would be soon in any case.

They weren't allowed to carry out that part of the plan, but it was an interesting sidelight on men and manners. They had one shallow grave dug, and placed a wounded man in it before Jeremy called my attention to it, placing the man so as to sit upright with his back against the end, and the victim seemed to take it all as a matter of course.

He would probably have died of thirst, if the vultures and hyenas didn't hasten the process; and in spite of that prospect he seemed surprized, and even resentful, when Jeremy ordered him carried up and laid in the shadow of a rock beside his own wounded.

He was bad-tempered, too, about the water that was given him to drink, swearing it wasn't fit for camels; and he cursed like a wet cat at one of Jeremy's men who was told off to bandage him. The other wounded were the same — indifferent to the prospect of a thirsty death in an open grave, and bitterly resentful of attention.

There wasn't much you could do for the wounded anyhow, and I wouldn't have cared to change places with them. They were slung on to the camels — one man nearly upside-down in a gunny-bag until Jeremy interfered — and taken along on the off-chance of their having enough stamina to survive the march; in which case they would be held for ransom, or else traded against prisoners held by the surrounding Sheikhs.

One way and another it was nearly an hour after the surrender before Jeremy provided me a camel and I started off beside him at the head of all his men to resume touch with Grim. The march, though, didn't seem to last five minutes, for Jeremy was garrulous, chatting away to me in English just as if I weren't pretending to be an Indian and disregarding my protests with a fine air.

"Make any explanation you want to afterward. I'll back it up, and they'll believe me, for I'm a great magician in these parts, mind you, and anything I tell 'em that isn't in the Book gets written into the appendix quick! Say, I haven't talked English for a century, it seems like, and I'm going to do it now or bust. You listen, and tell me if I've lost the knack!"

YOU MIGHT AS WELL have tried to stop the tide with a tin bucket. He talked away like a boy just home from school, and made you laugh because of the incongruity of all that flow of speech from a man dressed like an Arab, mounted on a camel in the midst of all that silent desert. The black cock's feather stuck into his brow-band was the only thing in keeping with his conversation.

"Yes," he said, "I've stuck to the old sky-tickler. Had to have something to remind me I was white. But say; as I was telling you, that fellow Grim's a two-legged man on feet. He has my vote. I fell foul in Akaba of one of those red-throated fools with inky fingers that the army calls staff-officers, and he was for having me treated with field-punishment number one plus. But Grim's white, and thinks without moving his lips. He said nothing, but slipped me away with a column of camp-roustabouts who left that afternoon with odds and ends of supplies; but I'll get that red-throat some day!"

"No you won't, he's dead. Died the same night."

"You don't say! Well, that's too bad. I was for getting my discharge in proper shape and going round the world to bust him in the nose. He called a beef-bullock an ox, and said I couldn't talk King's English. Well, he's in Hell now, and let him roast! He'll know what beef is when the fat runs! As I was saying, I slipped away with a column of fly-by-nights, thanks be to Grim, and they and I were fast friends in half o' no time. I did tricks for 'em, and they had me down for a number one wizard who should bring them luck.

"They'd made up their minds to cut and run with the swag before ever we started, and instead of slitting my throat they made me prisoner and had me giving a performance at every tin-pot village we spent a day at. We traveled nights, you know, and only looked in at the one-horse stands, where they hadn't enough fighting men to hold us up."

"How far did they take you?" I asked him.

"My God! We went forever! And I got so sick of finding money in a pocket-handkerchief and turning bullets into eggs that I began to invent new tricks, and got good at 'em too. Ventriloquism went over best, and I got to making he goats say their prayers and prophesy rain; and one day rain came after I'd done that, so they sacrificed the goat on a rock to Allah and made me a saint of El-Islam or some such tommyrot.

But they wouldn't let me go. A Johnny-on-the-spot who can make goats tell when rain'll come looked good to them, and they offered me a quarter-dozen wives, but no return ticket."

Being circumstantial godfather to Jeremy, I had my rights. I asked the obvious question.

"No. I'm a bachelor right down to this minute. They lined up a lot of 'em and offered me my pick, and some were not half bad. But I've kissed a few of the other kind, and I'm no King Solomon. The Queen of Sheba couldn't corral me! Crikey! Wait till I set foot in South Aus! One look round at the Bull's Kid, and then the wallaby trail, with soft grass under me!

"I'll take a tin billy and an old blue blanket for the love of it; and I know places where the little stations line out one by one along the road, and real girls in lilac and white sunbonnets and straw hats lean over the hitching rail at dinner-time to see if strangers are in sight who'd say yes to a meal. Oh, bully boy! Real women, with violet and blue and gray eyes, and red lips, and a jolly laugh! Say; you ought to come with me. I'll show you lips worth kissing if you'll take those whiskers off!"

"Thought you had a gold-mine?" said I.

"So I have. But how did you know?"

"Grim told me. Go on talking."

"Well, I got sick of it and hit the trail southward — stole a good camel and lit out one night with nothing to guide me but the stars and a habit of being lucky. North would have been best, but seeing I couldn't make that the south had to do instead; and the farther I went south the easier it was to beat my way by doing tricks. I got all the way to Yemen, and if a crow flew backward to keep the sun out of his eyes, he'd make a thousand miles of that trip even so."

"Weren't you sick by that time?"

"Uh-huh. Boils. Too many dates and muck like that. I needed a refit sure enough, but all I got wind of down in Yemen was another of these here staff-officers acting like the Devil in a small way near the coast, and if I'd gone to him he'd have had me pinched for a deserter sure — which I wasn't, but I couldn't have proved it.

"Top o' that I'd picked up information on the way down — white quartz, old son, with nice soft yellow veins in it that you could pick out with the blade of your knife; so I tossed up whether I'd hunt the home of that stuff or give that staff-officer a chance to call me names, and punch his head for it and go to jail. I used an old two-headed penny that I keep for doing tricks with, and tossed three times to make sure. Then I hit the trail again — north this time."

"Sick and all?"

"Why, no. I got feeling better soon as that penny made my mind up; and then I ran into an Indian doctor who'd gone broke in Mecca and was working his way home. That lad did me no end o' good. He could make good strong physic out of weeds — stuff that 'ud shift the inside out of a tombstone; and another thing that recommended him to me was a half-pound of mercury he carried in a little iron box. He traded it against a dozen lessons in sleight o' hand, but I gave him at least two dozen, for he was clumsy — no surgeon — just a pill-and-poultice walloper. He could palm six coins at once and fool his own eye when I was through with him. That mercury looked good to me, and I wanted the *Miyan* to have his money's worth."

"Did you hike back all alone?" I asked him.

"No. Didn't hike, and couldn't have bought solitude with real money. There were fanatics in Yemen unattached — sore as boils against every Sheikh in sight, and wanted for minor crimes like murder and rape. They took a fancy to the tricks I did and approved of my reputation for saintliness; and seeing they were first-class foragers, and wouldn't let me out of sight night or day, I took 'em along after they'd fossicked a fine new camel for me that belonged to the wife of an enemy of theirs. This is the beast I'm riding now; pippin, ain't it?"

"How many were they?" I asked him.

"Eighteen to begin with. But we went up Arabia like a magnet through a sand-heap, picking up the iron in it on our way. And I laid law down. Bet your life I did! Any fanatic who hesitated to obey me got stripped stark naked on the spot and turned loose without weapons to rustle an honest living.

"Top o' that I worked the oracle, of course, all ways from the middle, spending all my spare time auguring on certs; and when the certs I'd prophesied came off they wanted to start a new sect or something, and have me archbishop. Time I reached this part of Arabia there wasn't much I couldn't do in the way of getting things.

"Natural-born who didn't know what truth meant were afraid to lie to me, for fear I'd find 'em out and turn their livers into hot lead. I didn't have to ask more than thirty thousand times before they led me to the outcrop — leastways, to where the outcrop had been. Solomon or somebody about a million years ago when labor didn't cost much had shaved the surface down, and there were tombs on top of it."

"I'll bet you didn't admit what you were looking for," said I. "You'd never have found it in a million years."

"No. I wasn't as raw as all that. I showed 'em a piece of quartz

I'd won from a *m'allim,* who admitted it came out of a tomb; and I told 'em I was looking for a stone that would be holier than the black one in the wall of the Ka'abah at Mecca. I said that chunk I carried was a piece of it, and the fools 'ud come and ask to kiss the handkerchief I had it wrapped in. Well; I used to get so sick of asking questions that now and then I'd almost decide to head for Jerusalem and let 'em call me a deserter; but that was when I'd run out of the Indian's physic and my liver wasn't working good.

"I made some more physic by-and-by out of weeds I found, and took a chance on it; tried it on a sick Arab, and he got well, so I drank about a quart — it was awful bitter — and it fixed me to beat clock-work. Never had a sick minute after that.

"Say; after I've made this gold-mine pay I'm going to form a company and float that physic on the market — thought of a name for it too — name and a slogan — Jeremy's *taib,* tickles your liver and makes it laugh! Pretty good, what? Make a million out o' that easy."

"Tell me some more about the mine," said I.

"Oh, the mine? That's simple. There were graves on top of it, and they told me only one man had been down into 'em for centuries. That 'ud be the *m'allim* I won the piece of quartz from. So I did a bit of prophesying, and voted myself chairman of an investigating committee of one, to go down with a torch and tell the dead men what was going on in the world.

"We had a corroboree on top first, and they all did two-bow prayers, and I hadn't been down in the first tomb fifteen minutes before I struck it rich. Say; those old-time emperors knew how to make the hands turn to all right! D'you know what they did? You'd never guess. They took out the whole reef in chunks and shipped it — must have done! There isn't a sign of a furnace, or a mills or a dump. They took no chances on the local manager, but toted every bit of rock on men's heads to the coast and roasted it elsewhere. There's no other way of explaining it. And why they quit beats guessing. Maybe there was revolution. There would have been if I'd been one of the labor gang!

"They quit with the reef cut square across and the prettiest veins you ever saw — loaded, man, loaded! Running downward nearly due east at an angle of fifteen. I let on that the dead men down there wanted all the quartz removed because the holy stone I was after was somewhere underneath, and the only difficulty after that was tools and dynamite. You haven't got dynamite by any chance?"

"Grim knows where there's some hidden away. I've a drum of cyanide."

"I guess those whiskers of yours are singed feathers. You're a fallen angel, Ramsden! Who's that lordly-looking codger on a camel over there?"

"It's Grim," said I. "Seems he's coming out alone to meet us."

"The Hell it is? That Arab-Grim? Say; give me one o' your cigarets quick! I'm feeling nervous!"

And he was, too. His hand was trembling as he struck the match.

Chapter XI

"Allaho Akbar!"

COME TO THINK OF IT, that meeting between Grim and Jeremy was rather dramatic. I rode my camel to one side and looked on, keeping near enough to listen, but aloof enough to take in the whole scene — Jeremy's hundred in a long line two abreast, with the rear ranks closing up toward us like a telescope and all their spears and rifles pointing this and that way — Jeremy along in front, smiling with a strange twitch at the corner of his mouth — Grim facing him, sitting his camel square and upright, uncompromising as the Sphinx, and the sun beating down on the lot of us so hard that the dust devils, whirling in the simoom, shone with a glint of gold. The *fiumara* on our right hand, cutting the dry desert like a great wound down the middle. A horizon bounded by blue, hot hills. And Grim spoke first.

"Well, Jeremy, how's everything?"

"Oh, pretty good."

"Got a gold-mine, I hear."

"Sure. Want to buy a share?"

"Did you get the news of peace?"

Jeremy nodded and sat sidewise, swinging a leg across his camel.

"There's no amnesty yet for deserters," Grim said dryly.

"That don't faze me. See here, Grim; I'm no deserter, and you know it!" The old pugnacious look was dawning dark on Jeremy's face, but Grim paid no attention to it. He was going to lead his ace of trumps in half a minute, but you couldn't expect Jeremy to know that; it takes time to learn Grim's game.

"Got your discharge about you?" Grim inquired, as if he expected Jeremy to pull it out and flourish it.

"Say; you're talking like one of those staff-experts! What's come over you? Of course I haven't my discharge! How could I have?"

"Then you're still a trooper."

"Well? What of it?"

"Trooper Jeremy Ross of the Australian Light Horse, transferred on special service to Akaba."

"All right. Spell it backwards, if you want to! What's the game?"

"I'm Major James Grim, your commanding officer."

"Well?"

"If you're no deserter, you'll need proof of it. A court martial would summon me as witness. Being the first officer to get in contact with you, my evidence would be important."

"I don't get you yet."

Grim smiled broadly at last.

"Thought you were quicker-witted, Jeremy. What should the first act of a —"

"Oh, ha-ha! I get you. I report for duty, sir. Was made prisoner and kidnaped by deserting Arabs. Managed to escape, but haven't set foot yet on British territory."

"All right. You're ready to obey orders?"

"Um-m-m! Got a copy of the articles of war about you? I'd like to read 'em first. Is this a scheme to order me off to Jerusalem and jump my mine?"

"It's a scheme to save both of us trouble," Grim answered. "I'm going to give you an order. If you obey it, well and good; if not, you'll have to clear yourself as best you can without my help."

"Well; you were a white man when I knew you last. I'll take a chance. Go on then, sir. I report for duty."

"Are those your men?" Grim asked him.

"That's what they say."

"Make me and my party prisoners!"

Jeremy threw his leg back again and began to whistle.

"I'm not joking," Grim assured him. "I'm an officer on the strength of the British Army giving you official orders."

"Oh, all right!" said Jeremy. "Want to be crucified, or anything like that? We've all the extras."

"Suppose you get busy?" Grim suggested.

"Very good, sir. Major Grim, you're my prisoner! So are you, Ramsden! How many in your party, sir?"

"Twenty-three at present, including the Avenger's fourth wife, the Avenger's brother, a Sikh, and a party carrying supplies intended for you."

Jeremy whistled again and began to chuckle. "Better hand your weapons over, I suppose. And how about cigarets? If you've a packet of canteen gaspers in your kit I'll reduce your ransom!"

We each handed him a broken packet, and he almost lighted two cigarets at once, he was so glad to get them.

"Mind you, I'm not running a hotel," he warned us. "There's better hamper and dead sheep to be had in the Never-never country of West Aus; but if you've really got Ali Baba and my loads along, I'll feed you jam till further orders. Jam makes the grandfather goat slip down your gullet easier. And say, how about orders now? Who's giving 'em, I mean? Will you obey me?"

"My whole party surrenders to you and claims your protection," Grim answered. "We'll observe the conventions."

"Conventions, eh? You'll find me a stickler for those things! Dress for dinner you know, and no tooth-picks at the table — use both forefingers and a thumb to pull the gristle out of your back teeth. I think you'd better keep your weapons after all, because about the only convention we really observe is going tooth and nail for any armed party that crosses our landscape.

"There's sure to be a hot scrap between here and home, because the Willy-boy Avenger has it in for me; we've used up between us all the threats there are, like two dogs on chain. Something's due to give now, and you'll see the hair fly in mouthfuls! But, say; tell me the idea! What's the drift of my taking you prisoners?"

"Go to it first," said Grim. "I'll explain later on. I'm on the way to the Avenger's camp. First his wife and then his brother met me on the way. They tried to kill my escort, who happened to be Ali Baba's crew with your loads. You take the lot of us prisoners, and carry us off to your place. Isn't that clear?"

"Clear as bull-pen soup. All right. But who's the wife? Not Ayisha?"

"Yes, Ayisha."

"Golly, what a lark! She's been trying to marry me for weeks past. Come on, you prisoners, we're wasting time — lead me to the big feast! Oh, say, will the rest of you show fight?"

"No," said Grim, "I've warned them. They'll surrender."

"How about the Avenger's brother? He's a peppery customer from all accounts."

"Ali Baba will attend to him. Come on."

BUT IT TURNED OUT that Ali Baba had his hands full. The Avenger's brother never doubted that Jmil Ras had made the lot of us prisoners. In fact, knowing what his own men had been up to, and guessing without much difficulty how they had crept into the wrong wasps' nest, he was surprized that we weren't all slated for execution — but not agreeably surprized. There are lots of his kind. He wasn't a bit afraid of death, but he hated to surrender to a man whom he regarded as a rival of his brother for the overlordship of the district, and Grim's back hadn't been turned a minute before he was making Ali Baba all kinds of promises — heaven included — if the old man and his sons would desert Grim and make a bolt for it.

"But I said," said Ali Baba afterward, "by the tomb of the Prophet, said I, Jimgrim I know; and this world I have found good; by the grace of Allah I will stay in it and follow Jimgrim while I may. I die when Allah pleases, but not at the behest of a prince who sought to murder me an hour ago! And I said to my sons, said I, I am old, and it may be ye would like Mujrim for your leader now; therefore choose whether ye will follow me or this Avenger's brother, for my lot is cast with Jimgrim's and I wait here for him.

"So they came on the Avenger's brother from behind, and threw him on the ground, and tied him hand and foot; and Ayisha mocked him as he lay, until I bade the woman hold her peace."

The old man wanted to deliver all the goods to Jmil Ras there and then. Having no notion of Grim's ultimate purpose, any more than the rest of us had, he asked for a final settlement of accounts and leave to return home; and being a moderate old gentleman according to his lights, he only demanded a hundred camels for the mercury. But though Jeremy and Jmil Ras were one and the same man, their methods were as different as chalk from cheese — almost as those of Jekyll from the ways of Hyde.

"Did I not pay you?" asked Jmil Ras. "*Wallah!* You shall keep your bargain to the last letter of the last word in it! Your son Mujrim boasted to me that you dared follow any trail and fight whoever opposed you. Make good the boast, thou gray-beard! You shall fight your way to Abu Kem I promise you! Is it nothing that I meet you with a hundred men to help you keep faith with me?"

"*Il hamdul'illah!*" the old fox answered humbly, and added

almost under his breath with no humility at all, "curse you and your fighting! With me and my sons to help him, Jimgrim would have managed this without a fight at all!"

But I suspect that even he doubted the truth of that assertion within the hour. I don't know what plan Grim had had in mind before Jeremy arrived on the scene although I don't doubt he had one roughly formed that could be changed, as usual, at a moment's notice to offset the moves of any adversary.

But it is as certain as humanly can be that we should all have been in the Avenger's hands that morning if Jeremy hadn't turned up; and how Grim would have saved those goods from confiscation — which after all, didn't matter so much — and Ali Baba and his sons from death as traders with the Avenger's enemy — which did matter a great deal — beats imagination.

I've confidence enough in Grim to believe that he would have found some way out of the predicament, but I can't believe he would have settled the affair without a fight to the death between the forces of Jeremy and the Avenger.

As I have said before, the only rule that you can lay down concerning Arab warfare is that the water-holes are the all-important strategic, and whoever holds those can make the enemy come to him. Barring that, the strategy and tactics are haphazard, governed by a moment's whim and utterly confusing for that reason, so that the best-laid schemes unless put through with overwhelming force, are really more likely to fail against the Arab than some adaptation of his own rough-scrambled methods would be.

The Avenger had sent out his brother and thirty men to meet Grim, get those goods intended for Jmil Ras, and punish with death the men who had dared to trade with his mortal enemy. There wasn't any imaginable reason why he shouldn't have sent more than thirty men to accomplish that purpose; and if he had learned since that Jmil Ras was on the prowl with a hundred, there seemed even less reason why he should now send fifty more to reinforce his brother.

If he had sent two hundred, as he could have done, and had taken the field in person, he might have had a chance to catch Jmil Ras away from home and overwhelm him. An even sounder policy would have been to swoop with all his forces on the stronghold of Jmil Ras and take it by storm in the owner's absence.

But one bet at least seems safe — that most Arab chiefs will become hypnotized by the thought of possible plunder moving on the hoof. I suppose it seemed better business to the Avenger to make sure of possessing the goods intended for Jmil Ras, and the redoubtable Grim along with them, than to take his chance in a pitched battle.

And he may have been right, for all I know, because Jmil Ras, even with his back turned, was no easy mark for any man. Friend Jeremy had made his reputation good a score of times by out-generaling every leader sent against him.

Whatever the Avenger's argument, he sent out fifty belated men to re-inforce his brother, and they came down the bed of the *fiumara* two by two with all the serene confidence of men who expect to find the work already done. All the precaution they took was to throw out an advance-guard of four men, and Jeremy's lookout reported them before they came within two miles of us.

So we set an ambush in a hurry, which only worked suffi-ciently to draw the fifty within range — for the kites circling overhead betrayed us — and there was a first-class scrap that lasted nearly an hour and was better than anything that Colonel Cody ever staged.

You see, even after the kites had made them aware of us, the Avenger's fifty didn't know yet that we weren't exactly the party they had come to meet. They didn't even grow suspicious until their shouts weren't answered — and that was a mistake on our part; but Jeremy, who was giving all the orders, hadn't time to con-sider everything.

Sensing danger in time to escape the trap, they scooted up the back out of the *fiumara,* spread out in a wide half-circle, and came on to draw our fire. Half of them were mounted on mighty good horses, and the speed of their maneuver put us at a terrific disad-vantage for the space of about three minutes while we scrambled into new positions. If they had come straight on Lord knows what they might not have done to us; but, like the British fleet in the first attack on the Dardanelles, they didn't know. And it's what you do know that counts in the fighting business.

Narayan Singh, Ali Baba, Mujrim, and myself were the first to open fire on them. Jeremy and Grim had their hands full getting the rest of our crowd into a new formation to meet the emergency. An example was the thing most needed, for if too many people try to give directions in a crisis, circumstances usually take charge and the last state of panic is worse than the first.

And here I have a confession to make. I suppose it's a proof of weakness; and all the missionaries I have talked with on the sub-ject assure me I shall go to Hell for it. And yet — I wouldn't confess (for why should I?) if I couldn't do so without qualms. I hate to shoot a good horse. Grim agrees with me.

I've had to deal with men who see snakes in *delirium tremens,* but I never wasted much time swatting the snakes. It was simpler and more efficacious to deal with the cause of them. And so, as has happened more than once in my career, when a horse comes at me with a man on his back, rather than shoot the horse, who is hardly a free agent, I prefer to put a bullet through the man.

I can do that without compunction, because, to my way of looking at it, the man is a free agent and the horse no worse than a willing servant. Nevertheless, I've been called a murderer to my face by a missionary, who left three tied horses without water during two hot days and complained afterward about his own hard luck.

Well; there you are. I might have shot a horse, and that might possibly have had the same effect in the long run. But I picked out the leading man instead, and drilled him clean, and my three friends, crouching behind boulders on my right hand followed suit. I believe Mujrim missed, although he never would admit it, but at any rate, between us we tumbled three men out of the saddle, and one of them was dragged head-downward by the stirrup for half a mile before the horse stopped and came whinnying back.

That four-shot salvo saved an awkward situation for us, for the rest of the troop fired wildly from the saddle once or twice, wheeled sharp about, and galloped out of range, leaving the men on camels to make the next move. And while they thought about it, Grim and Jeremy had got our force straightened out, devised a plan, and got it fairly started.

Grim came running up with the rest of Ali Baba's men, and put me in charge of the lot, including Narayan Singh.

"Keep up a hot fire from here," he said. "Make them believe, if you can, that you're the main force. Don't spare ammunition. Don't move away from here; keep an eye on the Avenger's brother."

Having said that much, which was more than usual for him, for he doesn't often limit you, he went sliding down again into the *fiumara.* So I posted my men behind boulders and started up a rather long-range fire at the camel party, crawling from one man to the next to explain what was expected of us. Ali Baba snatched up the idea as a dog takes meat, and what with his croaking to his sons and my choosing one rock after another from which to fire several shots in rapid succession, I daresay we contrived a pretty good illustration of, say, fifty men at bay.

And neither the camel-men nor the horsemen opposing us dared approach the *fiumara* to discover how many we really were, or to take us in flank and rear, because of the possibility that we might have reserves down there in ambush.

Over my shoulder I saw Jeremy take most of his men, all mounted, straight up the *fiumara* in the direction from which the enemy had come. Grim, on the other hand, took twenty or twenty-five of Jeremy's crowd in the opposite direction, and in a minute or two the plan unfolded.

A QUARTER OF A MILE below us Grim led his small force out on to the plain, and the horsemen began to attack him mosquito-fashion, charging to within a hundred yards, to fire from the saddle, wheel suddenly, and gallop out of range again. I hadn't time to estimate casualties, for the camel party seemed to have made up their minds that our whole force was now accounted for and came at us headlong, yelling *"Allaho Akbar!"* shooting and flogging alternately.

But, you know, a man can't flog a galloping camel and shoot straight at the same time. They looked awfully ferocious, and I expect they would have scared the wits out of raw riflemen. They were brave, too, for I think they believed there were forty or fifty of us, and we had cover, whereas they had none unless you count the smokescreen of sand the camels kicked up as they came, which went billowing down-wind until you couldn't see what was happening in Grim's direction.

But you couldn't find a tougher, less easily stampeded gang in Asia Minor than the party Grim had left with me. They spat on their cartridges and crammed them in like veteran soldiers instead of the thieves they were by trade, and each bullet was loosed on its way with an appropriate curse, until Narayan Singh on the far right laughed so that he could hardly shoot straight. And the camels went down one by one like great ships sinking, pitching up their sterns as they plunged bow first.

But that war-cry *"Allaho Akbar!"* is something more than a formula. It seems to fire the men who use it with a frenzy that bullets can't quench. Camels fell, but their riders charged forward on foot, and by that time they could guess how few we were, which added confidence to fury. The amount of nickel-coated lead that a charging Arab can eat up as he comes is incredible. There isn't an animal — not even a bear — that can compare with him. That gang of fanatics charged home — got right into the middle of us — and used their knives to such effect that Ali Baba and his youngest son Mahommed were the only two who hadn't some sort of wound to show by the time we had beaten off their survivors. We were lucky to have none killed. Mujrim's devotion was all that saved old Ali Baba's life.

My share was a blow on the head from the back of a sword that knocked me nearly unconscious for a minute; Ali Baba came and bent over me — thinking I was dead — genuinely sorry I believe — but anxious to acquire my watch (which is an heirloom). Two men sprang on him as his back was turned and his fingers just beginning to explore my shirt; Mujrim laid them out, and fought a duel with a third, bagging three to his own knife.

Those frenzied Arab charges, though, are like oncoming waves that have to recede when the momentum fails. Unless they accomplish their full purpose at the first shock, they inevitably draw off and make ready for another and another, until there are none of them left to charge or the game seems hopeless.

I don't know how many we killed all told, for I was otherwise occupied when the time came for burying the dead, and Mahommed's song about it afterwards turned units into scores; but they left nine dead or dying among our clump of rocks. We had killed more than camels as they rushed us across the open.

The remnant ran at last as furiously as they had attacked, but by that time Jeremy's counter-attack was under way. He and about seventy camel-men swooped out on to the desert on the far right, cutting the line of retreat. I heard their roar rising in volume as they wheeled and started forward — caught sight on the left of the dust of horsemen reeling back in front of Grim — and that is all the account I can give at first hand of our pitched battle by the *fiumara,* for as my wits recovered from the sword-blow I recalled Grim's admonition to keep an eye on the Avenger's brother.

I looked about, but couldn't see him — couldn't see Ayisha either. They had been left close together in the *fiumara* just below the bank on top of which we took position, he tied hand and foot, and she glumly fingering her rifle — for she could hardly be expected to help us against her husband's men, yet couldn't rightly be regarded as an enemy.

Ayisha, to state it mildly, was on the horns of a dilemma. If we should be defeated and the Avenger's brother rescued, she would have to face that brother's charge of treason on her return home.

On the other hand, she wouldn't be much better off if we should win, for she would then be in the hands of Jmil Ras, who had rejected her previous overtures and who, if he followed the usual course, would merely use her as a basis of exchange, in which case there would still remain the Avenger's brother's enmity to face; for he was quite sure to be ransomed and set free along with her.

It would have been easy for her to murder him, and I haven't a doubt she weighed that idea thoroughly. But I dare say, too, that she took into consideration Grim's wholly incomprehensible — to her — but pronounced objection to throat-slitting in such circumstances; and she had a sort of reverence for Grim that I think came closer to being in love in our Western meaning of the word than any emotion she had ever felt.

At any rate, what she did do was to try the other prong of the dilemma first, and since she was dealing with another opportunist, it bent momentarily to suit her. She proceeded to make friends with the Avenger's brother — on her own terms, of course — and all the while that the fighting was going on she was negotiating with him the conditions under which she would cut the thongs that bound him and help him to escape.

If she could have been satisfied with just that, the two would have made their getaway and I would almost certainly have died before they did it; because it was after she had cut the thongs, and while the Avenger's brother was hiding between rocks, waiting for her to do the necessary scouting, that Grim's instruction to keep an eye on the two of them crossed my mind and I went to look.

But perhaps she wasn't any too sure of the newly purchased friendship. Most women in precarious positions have discovered that most men will promise them nearly anything in return for what they want at the moment, only to forget the promise when the time comes to repay; and though Ayisha was a most amazing optimist in some respects, she was cynical in others. She decided to take a magician with her to control events and conjure away mistrust, and I suppose she thought me too well attached to Grim to make the trouble of trying to persuade me worth the risk. So she crept up the bank, and lay beside Narayan Singh. And because she had her rifle along and made some show of opening the breech, he supposed that she had come to fight beside him against her own folk. A man hasn't much chance to think reasonably when the *"Allaho Akbar"* roar is rising and bullets fly; nor has he time to make hot love or be polite. He had to be coaxed a good deal and mighty tactfully before we could get his version of the story afterwards.

"O mighty fighter!" she exclaimed, as she watched him lay cheek to the butt and blaze away. "They told me you Pathans were only boasters, but *Wallahi!* are they all like you?"

"May the father of mistakes who made this rifle die of palsy!" he growled back at her — a little flattered, no doubt, although as suspicious as he had time to be. "I got the misborn weapon from the governorate at El-Kalil, and its vomit goes a mile wide of every mark! See that — may rats gnaw the eyeballs of the maker of the thing!"

"But you are a magician! Make magic, and the rifle will slay two men with one bullet!"

He had presence of mind enough even so to try to preserve that fiction.

"Magic takes a certain amount of time," he growled back, jamming in another clip of cartridges.

But Lord! She was quick to use another's argument as cement — and masonry for hers. "True!" she answered. "This is not your business. My lord is wasting time and running great risk at work that is only fit for thieves. Come away with me, and use magic, and you shall be a great chief! Come! Come quickly! Come and hide among the rocks, and slip away, and leave these cattle to their own devices!"

"Go whither?" He had time to spare for only two words.

"To Abu Kem, to the Avenger. He is a great prince, who will richly reward a friend. And have I not listened times out of number to my lord's protestations of devotion? Am I deaf? Can a woman's heart be like steel forever? Come now and show me how you topple down the thrones of kings!"

According to his own account Narayan Singh found time between shots to make her a tactful answer; but my private belief is that he called her *"Umm Kulsum,"* which is an opprobrious title, and told her to go to the good old-fashioned hot place that most of us would hate to think had been abolished. For then where could we send folk who don't like our points of view?

At any rate, she left him and went back to the Avenger's brother, and the two of them were conning their line of escape from behind a rock when I hurried down to look for them. It was only when Jeremy's attack began and our share in the fight was practically over that, fortunately for me, Narayan Singh grew really hot at the thought that Ayisha, or anybody else, should dare consider him corruptible. Anger increased suspicion, and he, too, turned toward the *fiumara* to discover what might be going on.

It was a big rock that the two of them were hiding behind. I looked around it, but they dodged me so silently that I didn't hear them. At the moment when Narayan Singh reached the edge of the *fiumara* and looked down, and I was on my way to investigate another clump of boulders, the Avenger's brother sprang at me from behind.

If he had knifed me to begin with I might feel differently about it, but he didn't try to use Ayisha's knife until he had tried first of all to pin my arms from behind and throw me. He said afterwards, and I believe him, that his first intention was to gag and leave me there; but of course he had no chance whatever of doing that to a man of my build and mere muscular attainments. I threw him forward over my head, but did not break his hold entirely, and he closed again, twisting round like an eel to face me.

It was then that he used the knife Ayisha had given him, stabbing me badly in the arm and following up by nearly braining me with the hilt. Coming on top of the sword-blow I got earlier his half-dozen hammer-strokes were too much even for my thick skull; but I didn't quite lose consciousness at once, contriving to clinch and lean my weight on him in the same sort of way that a beaten prize-fighter avoids being counted out.

But I got weaker every second, from the blows, not from bleeding — the cut in the arm was serious, but not enough to put me out of action — and if Narayan Singh hadn't turned up in the nick of time some other fellow would have had to tell this tale. It may be I've done Jeremy out of a profession!

But the Sikh did come like a landslide down the *fiumara* bank, swinging his rifle butt-end foremost, and the Avenger's brother had to take the heft of that on his collar-bone, which naturally broke. I was "out" by the time that happened — out; but, they tell me, still standing and clinging to my opponent; which may be true, but I think they lied to make me feel better about it afterward.

Chapter XII

"Ross, Ramsden, and Grim.
Grim, Ramsden, and Ross."

I RECOVERED consciousness in a most extraordinary place, where they had laid me because it was cool, and my head along with the rest of me seemed to be immersed in Hell flame before I was properly dead. As I came to I thought I heard war-drums near at hand, but that turned out to be nothing but my own pulse beating, although it was an hour or so before I realized the fact.

At the end of a century or so, that may actually have been an hour, or even less, after I came to my senses sufficiently to realize that the walls of the cavern weren't on fire but that my head was aching, Grim and Jeremy came and stooped over me, holding lanterns. Maybe I smiled; I tried hard enough.

"Not dead yet, you blooming immortal?" laughed Jeremy. "You cat o' nine-lives! Why, you old son a gun! We carried you balanced on your belly on top of a camel, and you bled so much that the camel's flank looked like a sunset in Port Darwin! You've got no right to be alive! What have you done? Jumped your bail, or wouldn't the Devil have you? Well; there's no need for you to believe in reincarnation; you can make the same old carcass serve you over and over, but it's a shame to cheat the worms that way. Sit up, and take a drink."

They had to help me up, but the drink worked wonders. I don't know how many halves of one per cent it contained; but as I wasn't in the U.S.A., Hawaii, or the Philippines, the Eighteenth Amendment doesn't cover the facts in this story. I felt better as the poison, if you like to call it that, crept through my vitals, and presently was asking questions.

"You're in my mine, old top. How long? Oh, two or three hours. It's nine o'clock tomorrow morning now; we marched all night and nearly killed the camels, but Grim said a little extra speed might save your bacon, and the darned fool insisted you were worth the trouble, so here we are. No, we didn't make 'em all prisoners; three or four got away — the horses were too fast for us. The Avenger has got a machine-gun or two, you know, and we expect he has heard the news by this and is oiling the works for a bit of strafing in return. We're making plans to hold our end up, and as long as he don't turn out too many Sheikhs against us, you lay your money on this team, old son!"

He propped me against the wall and walked about with his lantern, doing showman. We were not in a tomb, but underneath one. Six enormous slabs of stone lay overhead, with their ends resting on a cornice hewn in the solid wall. A seventh stone, twenty feet long, about eight feet wide, and two feet thick, had either fallen or had been levered out of place, for it lay at an angle across one end of the cavern, with its upper end against the wall. Perhaps it broke in falling, for there was a crack extending from end to end; they had thrust pieces of wood into the crack, to serve as a ladder. That was to my right hand as I lay.

To my left, where the last great overhead stone fitted snugly into its appointed place, a wide, hewn tunnel began, having straight smooth sides that widened perceptibly outward. At the entrance, where the tunnel was narrow enough, the roof was neatly arched, which I suppose really puts a date to it, although I don't know enough archaeology to lay down law on that. Grim said something or other about the date that I've forgotten.

But the architect — for he was nothing less; he hadn't been satisfied with merely cutting out the quartz, but had left the mark of his orderly mind on everything he touched — had been no stickler for one style. He was as utilitarian as any builder of sky-scrapers on Manhattan.

As the tunnel widened and the overhead arc became too extended for safety, he had changed his system and cut nearly square, leaving finely rounded pillars down the middle of the tunnel to support the roof. He seemed to have cut the tunnel to the very edge of the quartz reef, leaving only patches of quartz here and there along the sides, where the reef had widened irregularly.

"Lord knows who he was," said Jeremy, "but I'll bet the old son-of-a-gun had a high-bridged nose and a chin like Julius Caesar's. He'd ha' done for the British Army, he would! I'll bet he inspected the finger and toe-nails of each gang as it relieved the last, and worked 'em day and night in twelve-hour shifts. Look at the holes in the walls for torches. And see this thing? It's a knout-handle; the leather has rotted away, but there's an iron loop in one end to tie the lashes to, and the wood's all shiny from the sweaty fist of the overseer.

"But that's not half of it. It puzzled me for nearly a week to find out why the polish on the floor was different on this side of the tunnel from that side; it's all worn smooth by men's feet — you can pretty nearly slide on it where it dips — but one side's smoother than the other.

"I doped it out at last that the fellow with the knout stood here by the pillar directing traffic — you can even tell where a generation of the devils rubbed their elbows on the stone. The gang returning light kept down this side to the right; coming up again with quartz rock on their heads they took the other side of the tunnel and produced a finer polish on the floor because they were heavier."

I asked him how long the tunnel was, and whether the reef showed signs of thinning out.

"Seventeen hundred paces. No, she's shaved off square across, and there are three parallel veins. I'd hate to tell you what she'll assay to the ton, for you'd call me a liar, and your head's too sore to be punched at present. Notice how fresh the air is?"

You can't notice everything at once when you've lain unconscious for a day or so, but now that he spoke of it the condition of the air did seem remarkable. There was even a draft.

"There's more than a mile of old tombs along the top," said Jeremy, "and every blooming one of 'em a ventilator! Here and there they're close together; in places they're a hundred yards apart; but there isn't one that hasn't a shaft let down through the floor as far as the tunnel, and there's only one way they could have cut them; they must have lowered a poor devil with a pick head-foremost, pulling him up by the feet when he had some loose rock. No doubt they strafed him with a knout between tricks.

"The Arabs hereabouts think those graves are holy men's, but my guess is as good as theirs, and I believe that once in so often the gang would get an overseer with a hunk of rock, or a pick, or something and the big boss would have him planted in state along the reef. All the tombs were sealed up. I opened them. Every blooming one was built with a permanent opening toward the prevailing wind. only a couple of inches deep from top to bottom, but two or three yards long. The tombs acted as sandboxes; most of 'em are half-full of fine stuff blown in through the ventilating slit by the simoom, but they're so cleverly designed that hardly a ton of sand all told has got down into the tunnel in centuries.

"I tell you, Ramsden, old man, we don't know how to mine gold nowadays. We're savages! Good Lord! Why, they made old Charley Simms a lord for inventing a turbine ventilating fan that pretty nearly kills the gangs below-ground; but this old cousin of King Solomon, or whoever he was, probably got knouted for doing a ten-times-better job without a fan at all! This old codger was a sure-fire conjurer; our modern engineers are clumsy boobs!"

Under the spell of Jeremy's enthusiasm I began to feel strong and, as a man will do with the fever on him, insisted on being shown more. And as neither Grim nor Jeremy had allopathic theories to prove whether the patient died or not they let me have my way, and leaning between them I saw a lot of the wonderful shaft before surrendering again to weakness and having to lie down.

But even so, the exercise did good. I have seen it work equally well with animals and men; and, though the doctors call me a "lay theorist," which is bad language camouflaged, I maintain that walking about, if you can do it, makes the blood function normally and reduces fever. I know it cleared my head, and although I couldn't stand I was able to go on listening to Jeremy.

"Now, see here, Rammy old top! we're friends, aren't we. I got you out of a Hell of a mess once in Germany, when you wanted to fight the Prussian army" (Can you beat that?) "and I enabled you to score off the provost marshal in Cairo. You owe me a good turn. I've been talking to Grim, but every time I press my proposition he comes the bally major over me. I can't argue with him man to man. The son-of-a-gun listens, and then tells me I'm a trooper.

"But you're not in the God damned British Army, so he can't play that game with you. We've got a mine here that's worth millions any way you look at it. You talk Grim round — sit on his head when you feel a bit stronger, and punch him until he sees sense — and we three'll be mining mates — keep it between us and clean up!"

I LEANED UP AGAINST the wall and looked at Grim, who smiled exactly as I have seen financiers do when I wanted money for a prospect. You know the attitude? The thing looks good; they know you're telling truth and keep your promises or bust; but they've got other irons in the fire — know things that you don't know — and nothing's doing. One of these days some fortunate billionaire is going to find Grim out of a job for the moment and hire him. There'll be a whole new chapter then to be added to the secret chronicles of high finance.

Most of us show our hands too soon. Jeremy always does, except when he is conjuring; and I nearly always do, although I know what a mistake it is. Grim shows his, if anything, too grudgingly. But he always wins. All he chose to do just then was to point out the flaws in Jeremy's proposal, like a banker with a would-be borrower in front of him.

"You see, Jeremy, as long as you're a trooper you can't do a thing."

"But you can!"

"No. I'm in the army. I'm not allowed to engage in private business."

"Well then, quit the army! Turn in your perishing papers! What are you doing in the British Army anyway? You're a Yank. Get out of uniform and get rich!"

Grim shook his head.

"Can't do that, Jeremy. The army can rub along without me, but I need the army just at present."

"Well then, to Hell with it! Ramsden can turn the trick. Let Rammy own the mine. He's white. We'll divvy with him on the q.t. until we both get our discharge, and draw up a deed of partnership afterward. I've dollied out enough gold to finance us for a fair start. We'll make the thing pay as it goes, and to the Devil with banks and the stock exchange!"

You may bet that my ears were pricked. You forget a headache and a sort of foolish feeling in the stomach, when the dream of a lifetime looks like coming true. Most professional prospectors hope eternally for a gold-mine rich enough to pay its way from the start, and I'm no exception. But Grim still wore the high-financial smile.

"There's no law in Arabia, Jeremy old man, that would let you work the mine or give you title to it. There's no mandate here yet, and no government that could take that responsibility."

"To Hell with all governments!" exploded Jeremy. "We'll keep the thing secret."

"Can't be done," Grim answered flatly. When some men say a thing is impossible it makes any fellow with sand in his gizzard just that much more set on accomplishment. But even Jeremy, born optimist and independent enthusiast, realized that Grim wouldn't talk that way unless he knew whereof he spoke.

"What do you mean? Why, I can make ten times your salary at the end of this shaft single-handed! You can't kid me there's no way of working the thing."

"There's a way," Grim agreed, "but not yet, because you can't possibly keep it secret. You've been quiet, haven't you? You've fooled the Arabs mighty cleverly with tales about a white stone you're looking for and dead men talking from their graves. Yet I knew about your mine even before you sent to El-Kalil for picks and shovels. I don't mean that I knew all the details, but I had enough information to make the trip out here worth while, and I'd have come in any case."

"All right. You're one who knew. Who else had as much as a suspicion?"

"Half a dozen people. Besides, I shall have to turn in a report on this. I'm on oath — Intelligence Department — the Administration trusts me to investigate rumors and turn in facts."

"You mean you're going to blab?"

Jeremy looked scandalized, and Grim laughed.

"Don't worry! There are may be a dozen excellent reasons why the Administration won't want this thing talked about. Imagine what it would mean if Ben Saoud in the south, or the King of the Hedjaz, or both of them got word of it. There'd be civil war within the week. Next, Mustapha Kemal, who needs money like the Devil, would horn in from the north. Then you've got the Zionists to think of, with all their political influence; and the whole horde of Levantine financiers, who'd start pulling Foreign Office wires. Better a million tons of TNT than a gold-mine in this part of Arabia just now!"

"But here's the mine!" said Jeremy.

"What are you going to do with it?"

"That's up to you," Grim answered.

"No 'tisn't! Damnit, man, the minute I make a proposal you remind me I'm a trooper."

"All right," said Grim. "Suppose we drop all that — forget that either of us ever saw the army — and settle this between us three?"

"Good! Now you're talking. Go ahead. Here's a mine worth millions. What do you suggest?"

"Close it down. Seal it up. Forget it for a while," Grim answered.

"What? And leave it for the first chink or Indian or Arab who stumbles on it to jump and treat me to a ha-ha! Think I'm crazy? I've got two thousand pounds' worth of the yellow stuff, won from the reef with my own two hands, that says I'm not!"

"Pull your freight, then, while you've got it, Jeremy. That's my advice. You can stay here if you like, but you won't last long; the rival interests will tear you like a pack of wolves, once the facts leak out, as they must sooner or later. Whereas Feisul —"

"Ah!" said I; for like a flash I saw Grim's meaning, although Jeremy didn't.

"They tell me Feisul's down and out," said Jeremy.

"He is and he isn't," Grim answered. "He's still in Damascus, and the Syrians have proclaimed him king. But the French hate him, and are watching their chance to turn him out. They'll do it, too. But Feisul has lots of friends, including most of us who fought behind him in the war."

"You bet!" nodded Jeremy. "Feisul's a white Arab. I'd fight for Feisul against the French any day of the week."

"Well; Feisul is going to be the ruler of this part of the world before long," Grim continued. "He'll have to bolt from Damascus, for the French have poison gas, and Feisul's army has no masks. But he'll go to Europe — I know that because I've discussed it with him — and he'll tell his own story where it will do the most good. The politicians will be powerless after that to do anything but keep the promises that were made to him as an inducement to come into the war on our side, because when voters know the truth the men in office have to watch their step."

"What'll they do, do you suppose? Order the French to reinstate him in Damascus?" asked Jeremy; and Grim and I both laughed, for that was as typical of Jeremy as anything well could be. He is a trickster with his hands, and an expert at ballyhooing the spectators of his magic, but he can never think of any but the shortest cut to whatever he considers reasonable.

"Hardly," Grim answered. "You and I might offer to punch another fellow's head unless he did the right thing, but nations don't act that way after a long war. They'll contrive to save each other's faces."

"What'll they do then?"

"Find a new throne for Feisul, and there's only one that's possible."

"You mean this country? Lord pity him!"

"I mean Mesopotamia. This will be an annex to it; and Feisul is the only man living who can straighten things out from the Jordan to the Persian Gulf."

"All right," said Jeremy. "Good luck then to Feisul. But what has all this got to do with my gold-mine?"

"If you keep quiet about the mine, old man, and Feisul is made ruler of Mesopotamia, he'll be the fellow who can give you title to the mine."

Jeremy brought his open palm down on his thigh with a slap like a gun going off.

"Don't you believe it! I'm no hand at politics, but I know better than that! If they make Feisul king, they'll send him back here hog-tied with agreements to give the oil concessions to this financial gang, the gold to that one, and the railways and rivers to some one else. Good-by me and any chance I might have had of getting title to as much as a tomb to be buried in!"

Jeremy's good-natured face was now a picture of chagrin. He was much too intelligent not to see the truth of Grim's contention, but that did nothing to dull the edge of disappointment. What with my headache, and liking Jeremy so much — to say nothing of the glamour of that mine, which is a glamour that gets you harder the oftener you experience it — I could almost have wept for him. You know, a fellow gets weak and foolish when his head has been beaten a good deal with a dagger-hilt.

But there was an expression on Grim's face that I had learned to recognize, and I knew we hadn't got the last of his opinion yet. What he had said so far was by way of barrage laid down in preparation for assault; he would unpack the punch in a minute. I felt sure of it, and as it turned out was right. So I shed no idle tears in Jeremy's behalf.

"Don't forget, old man, that Feisul's white, Grim said, with his eyes fixed steadily on Jeremy's.

"He might be an angel, without being to beat those politicians!" Jeremy retorted. "Didn't you say you know where there's dynamite hidden? I'm going to blow the blasted mine to Kingdom come!"

"How about giving it to Feisul?" Grim suggested.

"What? Say that again!"

"Just now you promised to give it to Ramsden and trust him to divvy up afterwards. Why not treat Feisul that way instead?"

"What? Me partners with a king?"

"You and Ramsden. Why not?"

"Say; now you're talking again! D'you suppose — Oh, but

what's the use of kidding at a time like this? Let's blow the mine up. How much dynamite is there in that cache of yours?"

"You see," Grim went on, "if you and Ramsden were to go to Damascus and see Feisul — I'd give you an introduction — and if you were to tell him about this mine of yours and make him an offer, his hand would be a whole lot stronger when the time comes to deal with those political financiers in Europe. He won't have to give concessions in return for cash, or bargain away a shred of independence.

"What's more, if he has this mine to draw on he won't have to tax the Mesopotamian Arabs to the point where they rebel. And I know Feisul. He's a fellow you can bet on. All you'd need do is to get his signature to an agreement giving you the right to work this mine on royalty, and when he's made king he won't go back on it.

"It's the only chance you've got, but it's a chance to do more than make a pot of money. You'll be helping put the right man in the right place, and you'll spike the guns of half the money-pirates of Europe."

"And I'd rather do that than eat!" said Jeremy piously.

"Well?" Grim answered. "What about it? It's up to you, as I said in the first place."

Jeremy crossed his legs in front of him and knitted his brows, rather like a terrier puzzled by a blank wall. He thought, and scratched his head, and smiled for several minutes, and chuckled finally, as I had seen him do years before when a more than usually smart performer did a sleight-of-hand trick better than Jeremy's own.

"But who's going to engineer the closing of the mine?" he asked at last. There was a new-old light in his eye now, and Grim not only detected it, but understood it.

"You," Grim answered. "Who else?"

"Um-m-m! Might be done. Can do, as the chinks say. How much cyanide did you bring?"

"A whole drum. A hundred pounds of it," said I.

"Well, see here; if that fellow Feisul comes the king at me, and tries to treat me as a trooper, Lord love him, for he'll need it! I'll close the mine, and make Feisul a fair offer. If he accepts it, well and good. If he says no, I'll come back here and play a lone hand. But if he tries to trick me with promises and fair words, or gives me as much as a suspicion that he means to jump my claim when the time comes, I'll kick his royal backbone out through the jewels in the crown he wears for a hat, and they'll have to round up another emperor for Mespot. Rammy, old top, you and I once kicked a Prussian colonel; will you double up with me again and hold a king while I put my boot into him?"

I nodded, not that I had any doubt of Feisul; whoever has met him, and isn't a Frenchman with ambition to turn Syria into another Algeria, respects that man and trusts his given word. But I would play a busted flush against four kings for Jeremy's sake.

"Better soak me with the responsibility," said Grim. "I know Feisul better than either of you two fellows do. Jeremy doesn't know him at all, except by hearsay. I'll endorse Feisul's paper in blank, as it were."

"Meaning exactly what?" asked Jeremy.

"That if Feisul breaks his word to you, we'll reckon it as if I'd broken my word. In that event I'll let you name the penalty."

Jeremy grinned hugely.

"All right, old top, I'll name it now. We'll play this like one of your U.S. election bets. If Feisul makes a bargain with me and breaks it, you quit the army and come to Australia as junior member of the firm of Ross, Ramsden, and Grim. You start at the bottom as office boy — lick the stamps — polish up the brass plate on the door — argue over the phone with central — live for a year on thirty bob a week — and don't get promoted to a partnership until we own a mine as good as this one!"

"And if Feisul makes you a promise and keeps it, what then?"

"Why, then we'll be Grim, Ramsden, and Ross. Rammy's head ain't delivering its rated horsepower just at present, so he can't say no to anything. You'd better not try, Rammy; there are several sore spots on you that I could land on!"

"Very well; we'll call that a bet," said Grim. "Shall, we write it down? But remember, I don't guarantee to join the firm unless I lose. If I win, I have the option to become a partner. That right?"

"Sure. Senior partner if you win."

Jeremy wrote down the terms of the bet in Grim's memorandum book, and though he would have it that my brains weren't functioning, it was I, not he, who detected a ringer in our woodpile.

"Feisul's good faith is a cinch," I said, "but how about that report that Grim must turn in at headquarters? Are you going to cook it, Grim?"

"No, sir."

"Then what? Suppose some snooping office clerk gets hold of it? He could sell his information to a Levantine, or in London,

Rome, Paris — anywhere. There'd be gangs with some Foreign Office pull out hunting for Jeremy's mine like cruisers picking up a derelict; and if the Arabs tried to prevent 'em there'd be a new war, that's all. How are you going to keep your end of the secret, Grim?"

"Easy enough," he answered. "I report direct to the Administrator. He'll have to share the confidence with his Chief of Staff and three or four others; but every single one of them is pro-Feisul. There'll be nothing put in writing beyond a bald, and rather vague account of my journey to this place. The Administrator will send a private report to London, but if he calls this mine "ancient workings," such as are known to exist all over Arabia, that will only interest the archaeologists. And if he adds that steps were taken to prevent desecration of ancient tombs by private, adventurers nobody will be in any hurry to investigate. There's only one chance for a leak that I can see."

"Then sit on it and keep the water out!" said Jeremy.

"That gold that you sent to El-Kalil. It was bought by the bank in Jerusalem."

"There's going to be more of it, too," said Jeremy. "I'm going to take a bagful of the stuff away with me, and cash it in, for I'll need money."

Grim sat tight and looked puzzled for several minutes, like a player studying a chess-board.

"We'll manage that all right," he said at last. "Didn't you come here all the way from Yemen, Jeremy?"

"Sure did. Got fifty witnesses. Ask some of my bob-tail following. Pick out the lads who had to hoof it while I rode a camel."

"Well, we needn't lie about it. We'll contrive to tell the truth to any one who's curious in such a way that he'll conclude you brought the gold from Yemen."

"And that's a thousand miles from here," remarked Jeremy rather boastfully. But I think that if I had accomplished this feat I might be tempted to boast too.

Grim pocketed his memorandum book with an air of having closed a satisfactory deal.

"So that's all settled. Good. Now let's put Ramsden back to bed, and go and look at the defenses. If I know the Avenger — and I think I do — he'll come for us with all he's got. Just at present he'll be rounding up some other Sheikhs to help him; but he'll come quick before their enthusiasm wanes. Let's go."

"Lord! This is the life!" laughed Jeremy. "Sundowner one day.

Millionaire mine owner the next. Now turn politician and shuffle thrones — me that would kid a king as quick as look at him! Suits me all right! Come on."

Chapter XIII

"Oh, I say!"

I MADE THE SWIFT recovery that men of my type usually do. It is the ultra-sensitive and subtle-minded fellows who linger in bed after an accident; the less abstract the mentality the quicker its recovery, until you get away down in the scale to the lobster and the lizard, who can grow a new claw or a tail without troubling the doctor.

I lay through the day, but was tired of inactivity by nightfall; and even though the Avenger's brother with his broken collar-bone, and Ali Baba and Narayan Singh all came and talked with me on Jeremy's roof under the stars — for they weren't allowed into the mine and knew next to nothing about it — I had a hard time to idle through the following night, and dawn found me, if not yet fit for work, still less fit for doing nothing.

The Avenger's brother — his name was Achmet by the way — took quite a shine to me because I didn't resent his blows on my skull. But unless he had used the blade or the dagger first and killed me from behind, I don't see what else he could have done, do you? He had a perfect right to try to escape, and I was looking for him on purpose to prevent that very thing.

It wasn't a case for resentment at all; and besides, he had much the worst of it, for his broken collar-bone had pierced the flesh; and the wound, together with Grim's and Jeremy's amateurish surgery, caused him a lot of pain, which he endured, however, like a man.

"I will see that your life is spared when my brother comes, Ramsden Effendi. He will deal with Jmil Ras as with a scorpion that he crushes underfoot," he assured me. "But you and

Jimgrim shall be set free, because Jimgrim is his friend and you mine."

At that old Ali Baba snorted like a blowing grampus. He and the Avenger's brother were hardly on terms at all, and only tolerant of each other's company because there was no alternative. Ali Baba was really acting jailer, although he did not emphasize the point; as captain of our gang he ranked next after Grim and me, so Grim had chosen him for the task in order to show as much respect toward the Avenger's brother as was possible in the circumstances.

"Wait and see!" Ali Baba advised, nodding his old head sagely. "You think that the Avenger can sweep all before him; and he certainly must try for his own honor's sake. If he doesn't try to destroy Jmil Ras after this, his own men will laugh at him. But Jmil Ras holds Jimgrim, and Jimgrim has the brains."

"What of that?" the Avenger's brother sneered. "A prisoner can be made to talk; he can be made to work; he can even be made to fight grudgingly against his own side; for few men suffer torture very long without yielding up their will. But who knows how to make Jimgrim think, or how to make any prisoner think? Can you make me invent for you a way out of your difficulty, and teach you the way?

"No! Neither, then, can Jmil Ras make use of Jimgrim's brains. Make thy peace with Allah, Oh ancient of days, for the Avenger will tie thee to a gate-post in the sun, and where the ropes cut the skin the ants will enter!"

"Jmil Ras has bought Jimgrim," Ali Baba answered. "Gold is the stuff that can make a prisoner think."

"*Mashallah!* My brother the Avenger has more gold than Jmil Ras, and Jimgrim must know that."

"Maybe," Ali Baba retorted. "But he is meaner with his gold. This fellow Jmil Ras acts like a prince. He has paid me my price and the half again added to it. He will buy Jimgrim in the same manner, and you shall see a plan born, that will leave Jmil Ras contented, the Avenger obedient, and Jimgrim smiling; because that is Jimgrim's way. I know the man. *Wallahi!* I am the cleverest thief in all these parts, yet Jimgrim had the better of me; and if he can do that he can trap and defeat any ten Avengers! Wait and see!"

And then came Ayisha, equally a prisoner and deprived of her rifle at last though not of liberty to come and go within definite limits. She looked askance at Narayan Singh and laughed openly at me.

"Aha! *Miyan,* little use was thy magic against a man's blows! A *millieme* for such magic! And the other great magician had to use a butt-end to protect you! Bah!"

She evidently shared the opinion that the Avenger would come presently and capture the lot of us, and had made up her mind finally as to which side her own bread was buttered. She went straight to the Avenger's brother and rearranged his cushions, re-wetting the sponge under his arm, and doing all she could to keep his favor.

It was well that she chose that course, for though her forecast of events was wrong as it turned out, it would have been awkward for us, and worse for her, if the Avenger's brother hadn't approved of her.

There are much more pleasant fates than that awaiting a disloyal woman in Arabia, and simpler tasks than finding a new husband for Ayisha.

We certainly couldn't have left her to her fate, if the Avenger's brother had seen fit to charge her with treason; but she had another shot in her locker yet, and took good care before the climax came to establish her position.

Grim spent all that night alone on the same roof, but aloof from us, "thinking fish," as Jeremy expressed it. Did you ever see a Cape Cod schooner captain go into a brown study for hours on end "doping out" where the cod will go to feed next? All born fishermen acquire ability to do that; so do big game hunters; I have astonished myself more than once after a long spell of camp life and shooting for the pot, by an uncanny ability to reason out where the game will be at any given moment.

Grim, I think, applies the same sort of mental process in dealing with human problems. He seems able to withdraw himself from immediate surroundings and to think as Arabs do — exactly like a schooner captain thinking fish — with the result that he knows in advance what they will do without their telling him, and can make use of his knowledge either to assist or confound them.

In that respect he's exactly the opposite of Jeremy, who stages his play on the spur of the moment as a general rule, confounding all adversaries by a combination of quick wit and pugnacity. Compared to either of them, I'm slow-minded — slow on my feet, too, having to make up for that by a kind of patient tenacity — a sort of heavy siege-gun of a man, more often than not exasperated by my own inability to size up situations quickly.

I DON'T THINK Grim slept at all that night. The roof we were on was the usual flat stone affair with a coping all around it — about the only roof in all that village that hadn't needed patching when Jeremy pounced on the place. The house underneath it, strangely enough, was in ruins, the second floor and one of the walls having almost totally collapsed; but the roof provided a good view of most of the country-side, so Jeremy had made it his watch-tower and called the comfortless barn underneath, headquarters.

From time to time Jeremy's snatches of song and his leisurely cavalry footstep broke the silence as he came to report to Grim some information brought in by a spy, or to ask advice about a change in the defenses; for, though I expect friend Jeremy would have resented deeply anything that smacked of interference, he is no such fool as to neglect opportunity; being told to do things, and getting good counsel when you ask for it are as the poles apart, especially if you're Australian.

It was on Grim's advice, re-inforced by mine — for I'm a cautious man, not caring to bite off more than I can reasonably expect to chew — that Jeremy cut down ruthlessly the area he proposed to defend. The ruined, patched-up village lay on the spur of a mountain, whose true name nobody knew, for only the goat-herdsmen pretend to local knowledge of geography, and though they can always find their way among the hills, and each height and ravine has a name as old as history, no two of them ever apply the same name to the same place — which adds variety, of course, and is a gorgeous ingredient for building lies, but annoys us matter-of-factish Westerners.

It was a rather straggling village. That long line of tombs interfered with its formation, there being a Moslem prejudice against digging foundations too near to ground made sacred by dead men's bones. Months ago Jeremy had joined up house to house, pulling down the worst ruins for material for his wall; but the egg-shaped enclosure thus contrived was too big for the three hundred men at his disposal, and the greater part of the night was spent in flattening one end of it, as well as in improving the roof stockades, so that an enemy seeking cover behind outlying ruins could be raked from more than one angle.

Totaling up, we had water enough to last forever; food enough for about three weeks, after which we would have to eat starving camels; about a thousand rounds of ammunition to a man — Jeremy having raided the supplies of more than one local Sheikh — and men who did not deceive themselves with any hope of quarter from the Avenger, and who would consequently die, if need be, in the last ditch.

On the other hand, the news brought in by Jeremy's spies was not reassuring. In the first place, the Avenger's city, as he called it, of Abu Kem was only twenty miles away; so he had a perfect base for operations and could launch his attack without being hampered by a long supply train — the bugbear of all who take the field. Added to that, there wasn't a Sheikh within fifty miles who hadn't been annoyed by Jeremy in one way or another, and though the Avenger was far too ambitious to be popular, and too powerful to be trusted, a common cause will unite the most suspicious rivals for a while, and Jeremy had provided just that.

One spy after another brought word that the Sheikhs of neighboring villages were promising support to the Avenger. Promises don't always amount to much in that land, but there came information of night marches toward Abu Kem, and as the night wore on there were watch-fires lighted on the hills within ten miles of us. The Avenger's brother grew jubilant at sight of them, and vowed that he knew by their arrangement whose fires they were.

"Five thousand men will come against this place at dawn!" he said confidently, Ayisha nodding confirmation of his guess. "Better send messengers and try to make terms. Perhaps, if you surrender all the arms and all the loot, and if the men agree to forsake Jmil Ras for the Avenger, even the life of Jmil Ras may be spared. My brother the Avenger is no hyena; but, by Allah, he makes his name good when men oppose him!"

Coffee was brought up to the roof just then, and I made that an excuse for going over to Grim's corner and telling him what the Avenger's brother had just said. Grim nodded, and looked as if he expected me to understand the whole series of deductions that the nod meant.

"Out with it!" I urged him. "Coffee cuts grease; drink some and cough up what you mean."

He put his head on one side and looked up at me with a humorous twinkle, and a twitch at the corner of his mouth.

"He sure did batter up that bean of yours!" he answered. "Doesn't it occur to you that if he still thought Jmil Ras was an Arab he'd never have suggested sparing his life? Dog eats dog, you know. They're more bitter against their own heretics and schismatics than against any foreigner. That fellow knows his brother's mind pretty nearly as well as you know what's in your pocket. They think like twins."

"Well, what do you make of it? Is his opinion good news or bad?"

"You bet it's good. Guess I was tired or something. I've been puzzling the blamed conundrum and had it all doped out except for that one obvious point. Honest; it never occurred to me! You've put the key into my hand."

"Not consciously," I said. "I don't see the point even now."

"I've been figuring all the while that the Avenger would insist on having Jeremy executed for desecrating tombs and working magic." He brought his hands together as if sweeping the chessmen off a board. "The Avenger is mate in one move. Feisul wins!"

Well; I've overlooked a bet or two in my day. I went hungry for three days once, with forgotten corned beef in the locker; and on another occasion I forgot that you can make fulminate from cyanide and quicksilver, and wasted I don't know how many days waiting for detonators. And there was nobody in those days to give my tired-out thinking gear the necessary twitch, as it seems I did to Grim's. None the less, I can't help thinking that with all his mental alertness he would have found that loophole when the time came — as it did with disconcerting speed.

When the sun rose angrily above the skyline in a glowing smother of dust it was as if the vultures had been gathering overnight to attend our obsequies. There was no five thousand gathered against us — for Arabs exaggerate more wildly than the U.S. yellow press — hut certainly two thousand riflemen were bivouacked in sight of Jeremy's crude ramparts; and, what was worse, they had green banners with them, which implied that the real issue had been cloaked in a religious garb, so that we had fanaticism on top of greed to deal with. Jmil Ras had been denounced as a heretic impostor, and the sure reward of paradise had been promised to all who might die in the effort to wipe him off the map.

But no man living could take down friend Jeremy's colors by any form of threat. He came up to the roof grinning his usual boisterous greeting to the world at large, and using astonishing profanity in Arabic — which is a language all Australians ought to learn; it was built for hard swearing.

"Say, Grim, old top; Hullo, Rammy, come here half a sec. Looks like the last trick, don't it? The Devil couldn't lick that outfit with a matter of three hundred men! There's more on the way, too; that Willy-boy Avenger has managed to persuade his pals that I'm easy, and there'll be a race in a minute to see who can be first over the wall. We might stop half of 'em if the luck runs right, but Lady Luck looks sick at her stomach. Some of my last-ditchers seem to think there's more room over the skyline to dig the damned thing, and I'm offering two to one that half of 'em will bolt within two minutes of the first shot; the sons-of-guns won't get far, but they'll take their chance on that."

"What'd you think you're driving at?" demanded Grim.

"Why, this: you're my prisoners. Don't matter how or why, but prisoners you are and you've got to obey me. Anything I say goes; d'ye get that? Now I say, 'Get the Hell out of this! Take a man or two, look slippery, and hide among the rocks until this game's over.' Soon as they've scuppered me they'll quarrel among 'emselves and hurry off to loot each other's harems; then you hit the trail for Jerusalem. Now, no argument! You take and do what I say!"

He looked pugnacious enough, with his hands on his hips and head to one side, and I for one knew there would be a row before we could convince him, because Jeremy with his mind made up is less amenable to reason than a mule. But there came a diversion in the nick of time that brands me forever; and I don't know how to take the brand off.

Did you ever hit a woman? I did then. I hit Ayisha, and the weight of my left fist is no joke. The Avenger's brother was sitting on a pile of rugs and cushions in the middle of the roof, but I don't believe that he had anything to do with it. My judgment of the matter is that Ayisha thought she saw her chance to convince him finally of her loyalty. She was behind the Avenger's brother, and Jeremy's back was toward them. Grim and I were facing each other, with Jeremy between us in such a way that we naturally wouldn't notice much that might go on behind.

It was out of the corner of my right eye that I suddenly saw Ayisha spring to her feet and drive for the space between Jeremy's shoulder-blades with a knife about eighteen inches long. Lord knows where she got the knife; we had taken her own away from her. I knew it was Ayisha — never doubted that for a tenth of a second; and I didn't hesitate. I swung my left fist under the peak of her jaw and crashed her so hard against Narayan Singh, who was standing fifteen feet away, that the two went down together. There was no need to count ten. She was out; and she stayed out for several minutes.

"Oh, I say!" said Jeremy.

And Grim said nothing, which was worse. I pointed to the

knife on the floor and said nothing too, for I hate a man who makes excuses. Having done a thing it suits me as a rule to face it out; a course which doesn't make black white by any means, but at least doesn't add yellow to it. Jeremy ignored the knife, shouted for water, went and picked up Ayisha, and laid her on the heap of cushions close to the Avenger's brother.

Grim didn't waste a second then on side issues. He snapped into action like a piece of spring mechanism.

"Quick!" he said. "Before Jeremy gets back on the track! Remember you're an Indian now. Take Narayan Singh, and the two of you cross to the Avenger's lines. Tell him you've come from me — that I'm a prisoner — but that on my word of honor I can settle this to the Avenger's advantage if he will meet me in that old tomb half-way between our lines and his. Let him bring three or four men, and I'll bring three or four; and here, I'll give it you in writing; pledge my word that if nothing comes of the negotiations our side will take no improper advantage of him.

"You'd better tell him I've got Jmil Ras buncoed. You can also say that if he doesn't agree to meet me and discuss terms, I shall take the side of Jmil Ras and there'll be a fight then that will cost him the utmost damage I can help Jmil Ras inflict."

I was glad enough to get away from there, even on such a dangerous mission as that. You fellows who haven't ever knocked a woman down with your fist may not believe it, but it makes you feel like a yellow hound, even when by doing it you have saved the life of such a man as Jeremy. It would only have made matters worse if Ayisha had found me standing over her when she came to; for the more guilty a woman is, the more bent she will be on contrasting the iniquity of some one else. There would have been a scene that would profit nobody.

So I stayed not on the order of my going, but beckoned my good friend Narayan Singh and started down the outside stone stairs at just about the moment when the first irregular salvo of rifle-shots announced that one of the Avenger's neighbors on the far right had elected himself conductor of the overture. The range was much too long for effect, but among rival Sheikhs it is something to be able to boast of leading the men who fired the first shots.

"That was a good blow you struck, *sahib*," the Sikh growled in my ear as we reached the bottom of the stairs. "If it broke a woman's jaw, what odds? It saved a man's life!"

But I think that in his heart he, too, regretted that I had struck it. If I had thought twice I should rather have struck Jeremy and knocked him sidewise out of the path of the knife. However, it's no use arguing after you have done a thing.

Chapter XIV

"By Allah, it is too late!"

IT TOOK US LONGER to get past Jeremy's defenses than you might expect. They tell me that Australians are shock troops, rather given to despising precautions and bent on winning every fight by speed, bravery, and direct assault, with a quick-witted trick or two maybe thrown in now and then, just to prove what they can do when so disposed, but above all mockingly irreverent of every theory except one — which is, that Australia can't be beaten.

If Jeremy is typical, then that description of Australians is true. But perhaps he is unique, as his defenses surely were. They seemed to have been devised much less to keep out an enemy than to make it easy to sally forth and swat him.

There was excellent cover here and there for Jeremy's men, and the wall by which he had connected house to house was a good screen, but not much more, for there were gaps in it at frequent intervals, and where they were missing almost any man with hands and feet could climb it. I should say it was deliberately devised to tempt an enemy to attack without wasting time, but when I asked Jeremy about it afterwards he only laughed.

"Did you ever catch a showman telling how he turns his tricks?" he asked me.

Well; it was a chain of tricks that Jeremy had stretched around the place, and as it turned out it was I who had provided the star feature, but I did not know that at the moment. My head ached damnably, so I sat in the gap of a more or less unfinished wall and let Narayan Singh scout about a bit for some way of reaching the Avenger's lines without being seen by either side until we might choose to show ourselves; for there was just as much risk of being shot from behind by some of Jeremy's enthusiasts as of being plugged from in front by the enemy.

And while he did that I observed Jeremy and Ali Baba followed by Ali Baba's gang lugging a great iron pot between them headed for the northeast corner of the wall at the point where Jeremy had shortened the line he proposed to defend. Of all the easily assailable points that corner looked like the weakest, so there was nothing wonderful about his posting Ali Baba there; that old rascal and his sons would give a costly account of themselves against any odds whatever, and if there was a trick to be pulled off they were the lads who would pride themselves on managing it perfectly.

Narayan Singh spied out the route at last, and we crawled forward, but the oftener I looked back the less optimistic I became. Maybe the headache had something to do with that, but it seemed to me that if I were the Avenger I would attack that place rather than waste time talking.

Apparently the Avenger's temporary allies on his left wing shared my opinion, for they were following up their opening salvo by creeping closer, about four hundred strong, and taking up position to assault that obviously open corner where Ali Baba and his men were posted. There was nothing but a breast-high rampart of broken stone between them and our men.

So I hurried. If a fight could be prevented, the time to do it was while the issue was in doubt. It was a precious poor exhibition of scouting that Narayan Singh and I gave as we crossed the open ground toward the lip of the hill where the Avenger's black tent was pitched. We were seen when about half-way, fired at by a hundred men for several minutes, and were pounced on and roughly handled when we managed at last to hoist a handkerchief on a stick. The stick was shot out of the Sikh's hand before our surrender was accepted.

But they took us straight to the Avenger's tent, which after all was the main thing. And he, being a decent fellow after his own kind, cursed our captors roundly for having made us both bleed as they tore nearly all our clothes off. He did that even before he recognized me as the Indian who had accompanied Grim on that trip to Abu Lissan, when Grim got the better of him in a bargain.

"*Miyan*," he said then, stroking his fine black beard, "this is no way to have treated Jimgrim's friends. Those devils of mine shall pay for it. What brings you?"

So I told him, giving Grim's message word for word, and adding that Jimgrim was confident of being able to persuade Jmil Ras.

"By Allah, it is too late!" he answered. "Nine other Sheikhs have joined me to make an end of Jmil Ras, and who shall stop them now? Look; they haven't waited for my order. I can hold my own men for a little while, because they know that if we attack first those others will loot our baggage; but once those neighbors of ours are over the wall, my men will follow. *Inshallah*, let Jimgrim not be slain by accident. Is my brother well?"

He said nothing about his wife Ayisha, because that wouldn't have been good manners; but I said that a member of his honor's family had done her best to make his brother comfortable, and he understood me. After that he cut the conversation short, because the fighting over on the left had started in real earnest.

All I could see for it was to hope with him that no half-dozen frenzied fanatics would find Grim and kill him before he could be protected. I didn't have much doubt of the Avenger's good faith; all tales about him; and our own experience of him in the past were in his favor; and he looked the part of a chivalrous and honorable chieftain, as he stood there with his arms folded watching the progress of events.

It wasn't easy to watch. We had to screw our eyes up, because a scorching hot wind blew toward us. I know I wouldn't have liked the job of facing it on camel-back, let alone on foot against defended ramparts. The obvious course would have been to make a circuit and attack from the other side, when the odds would have been reversed and the defenders blinded by the dust and heat; but the rival Sheikhs were too impatient to begin.

I don't think our side fired a shot until four hundred madmen densely massed in nothing remotely resembling a military formation broke cover from behind low rocks yelling *"Allaho Akbar,"* and started to rush that weakest corner of the wall where Ali Baba lay hidden. And even then the firing on our side was feeble. It looked as if our men, with the dust and wind behind them and the wall in front, had lost heart already. There wasn't more than enough shooting to keep the assaulting force keyed up, and very few of them fell at first — not more than a dozen I should say — until a strange thing happened.

The hot wind increased in violence and the dust flew in a stinging cloud, but that hardly accounted for it, especially as the enemy rushed close and began to get a little protection under the lee of the low wall. But all at once they began to go down, face forward and writhing, numerically out of all proportion to the amount of firing from our side.

As the dust storm writhed and twisted it looked exactly as if it blasted them, until at least the half of the four hundred lay dead or struggling on the ground, and the remainder, covering their faces in their headcloths, turned and ran.

Then, and not until then, Jeremy's men opened up a really withering fire on them, raking and cross-raking them from the rear, and a murmur sounding almost like a prayer went up from the ranks of the Avenger's men.

But the attack wasn't over yet. There were other Sheikhs whose men proposed to show the runaways how real warriors attack a wall. Another roar of *"Allaho Akbar!"* broke out like a series of explosions, and eight hundred or a thousand men broke line to storm the whole line of the defenses. Not firing much — for the wind prevented that; they charged with their left arms held up to protect their faces and went like bolts into a sea of dust — they covered the intervening half-mile as if it were a race for money. And those on the right nearly reached the wall, making for the obvious gaps, where Grim and Jeremy directed a hail of bullets into them. There was hand-to-hand fighting in the breaches before the right wing of the assault reeled back.

But over on the left, where the bulk of the attacking force attempted to charge home and Ali Baba waited for them exactly the same thing happened as before. They went down in dozens and lay writhing, as if blasted by the dust.

"Uh! Poison gas," remarked Narayan Singh, standing on my right-hand. But I knew that Jeremy had no poison gas. How should he have? And on my left the Avenger expressed a different opinion.

"By Allah, that is magic! They have told the truth of Jmil Ras; he and the Devil are in partnership!"

But I could see the Avenger's face, and there was a look on it of something rather less poignant than chagrin. It called for scant mind-reading to deduce that he didn't exactly resent seeing his neighbors' forces decimated. If he could make favorable terms now his own supremacy in that part of the world would be unassailable.

"Do you think Jimgrim would come out and meet me now?" he asked.

"*Inshallah,* why not?" said I. "If he should see you and me and my friend here advancing alone across the open he would come at once to meet us."

"By Allah, we will try it!" he answered.

But he harangued his own men first, displaying the sort of political opportunism that a man needs if he is to be a successful ruler almost anywhere. I wouldn't call him a liar exactly, that being a hard word, and he a fairly good sportsman with the game not won; besides, our daily papers set him the example.

"Now, ye impatient fools!" he thundered at them. "Now do ye understand why I ordered you to lie still? See what I preserved you from! Ye would have met the fate of those fools yonder but for my wisdom! By my beard and the Prophet's feet, ye would be no better than the goats without me to save you from destruction! Wait now and guard the baggage, while I go and settle this affair without losing one man's life!"

"*Wallah!* You seem to have faith in your star!" said I when he returned to the tent with two men whom he had selected to go with us.

"I have faith in Jimgrim," he answered. "Jmil Ras is too many for me, but Jimgrim will know of a way out of it."

We waited a few minutes yet while word went down the line that all firing was to cease pending the outcome of negotiations; and the word hadn't passed a dozen lips before it was twisted into a report that Jmil Ras had offered to surrender. Some of the men began putting up a pole to crucify him on. But that was Grim's affair; he had said he knew how to extricate Jeremy from the mess. Narayan Singh and I followed the Avenger and his bodyguard of two straight forward across the open, walking slowly to give Grim a chance to recognize us through his glasses.

And as I had predicted, Grim came out to meet us. But he surprized me, nevertheless, for he brought with him Jeremy and Ali Baba to offset the Avenger's two; and after stately and very formal greetings we all sat down in a circle beside a battered ancient tomb that afforded shelter from the wind and dust. Jeremy nodded to me with the brightest twinkle in his eye you ever saw — "Thanks for the cyanide, old top!" he whispered.

"It was I who roasted it!" said Ali Baba out aloud, tapping his chest with conscious pride. "Did you see the devils wilt under the magic?"

Then the business began; and because Grim led off it was shorter and more directly to the point than any other conference with Arabs that I ever listened to. Grim's face was stern, although

Jeremy smiled all the while and kept up a running fire of jocular comments, mostly in undertones but now and then aloud.

"Now, O Avenger," Grim began, "I promised that if you should get into trouble I would come and help you in my own way. Here I am. Are you going to listen to me?"

"By Jimgrim! This is my country from the Gates of Petra to the border of the Hedjaz; I will listen, but none shall dictate to me!"

"We'll see about that," said Grim. "Would you rather listen to me or to Jmil Ras?"

"Jmil Ras is a wicked bastard, who must die!" he answered.

"*Taib!*" said Jeremy promptly. "Let you and me settle it together right here! Come on, I'm ready! Knives — pistols — swords — rifle — bare hands — if you want a piece of me, come and help yourself!"

"You talk like a white man!" the Avenger sneered.

"Well, what in the bloody Hell d'you take me for?" Jeremy retorted in English with a laugh. "D'you think an Arab would have let your brother live, or have respected your captured wife? You're a looney, that's what you are! Come on, old top; let's have it out and see who's the best man!"

"What does the madman say?" asked the Avenger; and his question put another weapon into Grim's hand.

"He is quite mad," Grim answered.

"Here — steady on, old top!"

"He is an Australian, whom Allah afflicted; but he eats out of my hand."

"Well I'll be damned!" put in Jeremy.

"He thinks he is damned, and therefore that nothing matters," Grim continued. "Being, as he supposes, damned already he is not afraid to open tombs or to make use of witchcraft and black magic; but he hasn't harmed your brother or your wife. He will listen to me. But if you won't listen to me, then I will simply leave him here and let him do his worst. If, on the other hand, you wish me to take him away there is a condition that you must agree to first, taking oath on the name of Allah, and by your beard and your own honor and the honor of your sons."

"You say he hasn't hurt my brother?"

"Your brother has an injury sustained in fair fight, but he has been treated with respect and is satisfied on that score. You may have back your brother and the other member of your family, who is unharmed except for an accidental bruise on the jaw-bone."

"By Allah!" chuckled the Avenger. "That may stop her talking for a while!"

"And you may have this place, and may take over all the followers of Jmil Ras —"

"Half a mo'! Half a mo'! Whoa, hoss!" said Jeremy. "There's ten of the blighters he can't have. Ten of 'em went underground with me and know the secret — or at least enough of it to give the game away. By crikey, they and I don't part company!"

"You may have all of his men who care to follow you, excepting ten, whom Jmil Ras himself will select," said Grim.

The Avenger's eyes were gleaming. The addition of about three hundred men to his force would be a victory in itself, for it would make his supremacy indisputable.

"By Allah, the condition! What is the condition? Name it!"

"You must agree to support Feisul. You must promise on your honor that when Feisul is proposed for ruler of Mesopotamia you will take his part with all your men and all the means at your disposal, receiving therefor proper dignity and treatment. And these tombs that have been opened —"

"*Wallah!* They must be closed again, and stay so! That damned Jmil Ras has brought enough sorcery out of them already to destroy the world! Have no fear about the tombs!"

"They must stay shut until Feisul opens them," said Grim. "Feisul is a direct descendant of the Prophet, who may do without harm things that other men may not do."

"*Taib.* But what if I refuse to support Feisul? I am the ruler of these parts. Let Feisul be king in Baghdad, and I will not prevent, but let him leave this part to me."

"If you refuse, you must fight Jmil Ras without my help," Grim answered. "I am his prisoner; I will return to the village with him and events must take their course. Perhaps you would like to send your men against his magic?"

"By damn, not I!"

"Then choose," Grim answered. "Feisul is a true prince, by blood, creed, honor, and action. You are a man of honor, too. Which is better: To be a petty Sheikh, with this thorn in your side, and the hands of the friends of Feisul all against you to insure your downfall in any event when Feisul's day comes; or to be the powerful supporter of a king, with proper honor and reward?"

"*Mashallah!* You have a tongue of silver, Jimgrim!"

"And what are your ears — leather?"

"Nay, they are golden! I have nothing against Feisul. Let him be king, if he can accomplish it."

"That is not enough. Will you support him?"

"On your terms, and if Jmil Ras goes, away, yes I will be for Feisul, if he can win the throne."

"Will you help him win the throne?"

"*Wallah!* What a persistent fellow! Very well, I will help Feisul."

"Do you swear it?"

"Yes."

"Let me hear you."

"By Allah and all His names; by the Prophet of El-Islam and all the holy saints; by the great Ali; by the Forty Martyrs; by my beard and my own honor and the honor of my sons, I swear to help make Feisul king, and to recognize him and support him, provided that Feisul recognizes me as first among the Sheikhs from Petra to the borders of the Hedjaz."

"All right," said Grim. "You have sworn before witnesses. As long as you keep that oath I'll be your friend. If ever you break it, I'm your enemy. Now shake hands with Jeremy Ross the Australian."

"Wallah! I would dread to do that. He is mad, and he has handled magic —"

"You can turn the magic away from yourself by shaking hands with him. Take my word for it," said Grim.

"By Allah, your word is good, but peace of mind is better! I would rather not."

But Jeremy had the solution all ready for that little difficulty.

"Put a bullet in the palm of your hand, and I'll give you a sure sign," he said, "that it's peace between us from now on."

The Avenger hesitated, but Grim urged him, and at last he worried out a nickel bullet from a new cartridge and laid it in the open palm of his right hand.

"Abracadabra!" said Jeremy. "Woolloomooloo! And three rousing cheers for my discharge!"

He seized the Avenger's hand, shook it once, and let go. The bullet had vanished, and a bright gold Turkish medjidie lay in its place, worth I dare say twenty U.S. dollars. The Avenger laughed.

"Can you do that always?" he asked.

"It happens as often as I make friends with a man," said Jeremy. "Don't spend that coin, though. As long as you keep it you're protected against magic. Now that I've made friends with you I'm going to stow the stuff that killed those fanatics yonder down into the tomb, and close it tight. And I'll put a spell on the tomb that'll keep the devils quiet. But if anybody except me, or Feisul, who's a direct descendant of the Prophet, dares to open the tomb, that stuff that killed those men will turn itself loose, and you'll all find Hell comfortable in comparison."

It's easy, of course, from this distance to laugh at the Avenger for a simpleton; yet I've seen people in New York, who had a college education, deceived by quackery equally absurd and without any such object-lesson as the Avenger had just witnessed. There were more than a hundred men lying dead or dying within a half-mile of us, who bore witness to the deadly efficiency of Jeremy's magic. I think it would have been a marvel if he hadn't been convinced; for that is a land full of ancient superstitions, where the tales are mostly about jinn and ifrits, who perform incredible miracles whenever it suits the plot.

The Avenger in my judgment is one of the most decent and manliest Arabs I have met; and having witnessed that verbal agreement between him and Grim and Jeremy, it gives me pleasure to know that be has kept his part of it religiously, although how and when he struck for Feisul must be told another time. We are most of us superstitious in one way or another, and it is wisest not to sneer at a decent fellow who believes in devils and black magic but keeps his given word, come one come all, through thick and thin. I'll doff my hat to him or his brother any day.

Chapter XV

"Ali Baba! Ali Baba!"

THE AVENGER'S MEN had to bury the dead, for the other Sheikhs cleared out in a hurry, taking their wounded with them, for they questioned their own safety now that the Avenger's force outnumbered theirs; and their men, having had enough of it, were unmanageable.

Jeremy buried the remaining cyanide and closed up the tomb that covered the mouth of the mine with ceremony that would have done credit to any stage in the world. He caused the voices of the dead to speak out of the tomb, confirming his threat of what would happen if anyone but Feisul or himself should dare to trespass in there; and he kept the ten men who knew the secret and had helped him dolly out the gold-dust standing near him, chanting a jingle he had taught them, while he himself did astonishing tricks of sleight-of-hand — pulling a live chicken in halves, for instance, and making two live chickens of it. There isn't a better showman in the world than Jeremy Ross.

We pulled our freight that evening. Thousands of successes have been spoiled by staying around to talk about them afterward. And besides, you couldn't have kept Jeremy Ross there another night without tying him hand and foot; he was like a boy released from school, dancing and singing and making a fool of himself until a saying started that they tell me has persisted until now — "as mad as Jmil Ras."

"Say, you chaps, come with me to Sydney! I'll show you the old Bull's Kid, and then we'll hit the grass trail — country where you can buy a horse for twenty pounds that can gallop all day long, and the girls have sweet red lips — Oh golly! I'm so sick of camels and the talk they sling out here that I'd swap my gold-mine for a billy and blanket and a six months' miner's right! Come, and I'll show you what life is!"

"What would you do with your ten Arabs?" I suggested, thinking that would faze him. But not a bit of it.

"Do with 'em? Why, take 'em along, of course. They wouldn't let 'em land in Sydney without a bond, but I've got money — and still more in the bank at home. I'll turn 'em into a traveling show — teach 'em tricks, and make their blooming fortune. They'll know where Allah lives when they've been in Australia half a day!"

However, that wasn't their destiny; there were other activities in store for Jeremy and Grim and me and them, as I hope to tell.

Meanwhile, our satisfaction was almost mild compared to that of Ali Baba and his sons. It was Ali Baba who had kept the fuel lighted under the great iron cooking-pot and sent the fumes of cyanide downwind, and his sons, who had defended him with rifles while he did it, were agreed that the honors were all his.

So Mahommed, his youngest-born, gang poet and sublime romancer, made up a song about it and they sang it on the march all the way home to El-Kalil. I don't remember nearly all of it, but I wrote down a few of the stanzas and have tried to translate them into English, though they lose most of their virtue in the process.

Who came out of El-Kalil?
Ali Baba! Ali Baba!
Bearing magic on his camels,
Ali Baba! Ali Baba!

Laughing scorn of the Avenger,
Making mock of all his numbers,
Giving confidence to Jimgrim,
Giving good advice to Jimgrim,
Ali Baba! Ali Baba!

He who rode from El-Kalil!
Who defeated the Avenger?
Ali Baba! Ali Baba!
In a battle in the desert,
Ali Baba! Ali Baba!

Conquered all the desert horsemen,
Made a prince's brother captive,
And rode on into the mountains
With his magic on the camels?
Ali Baba! Ali Baba!

He who rode from El-Kalil!
Then he mocked them in the mountains,
Ali Baba! Ali Baba!
And he called his sons around him,
Ali Baba! Ali Baba!

When a thousand desert chieftains
Swore to follow the Avenger
Bringing each a hundred horsemen
With their banners to attack him,
Ali Baba! Ali Baba!

He who honors El-Kalil!
But the father of fine magic,
Ali Baba!
Swore by Allah to destroy them!
Ali Baba! Ali Baba!

He, the friend of all the ifrits,
He, the brother of the lightning,
Took a cooking pot of iron
And he filled it full of magic!
Ali Baba! Ali Baba!

He, the pride of El-Kalil!
Then the thousands came against him,
Ali Baba! Ali Baba!
A hundred times a thousand!
Ali Baba! Ali Baba!

But his magic made a tempest,
And he loosed the tempest at them,
And he mixed the magic with it,
So that Azrael obeyed him!
Ali Baba! Ali Baba!

He who rode from El-Kalil!
So they cried out as they perished,
Ali Baba! Ali Baba!
For the storm of dust obeyed him,
Ali Baba! Ali Baba!

by Talbot Mundy

And he smote them in their thousands,
He, the father of fine magic,
And they fell and died in thousands,
Oh, he slaughtered them in thousands!
Ali Baba! Ali Baba!
He whose home is El-Kalil!

Well — that's how history gets written. Mahommed, son of Ali Baba, is another man without a college education, and as full of superstition as a Jerusalem mattress is of bugs; but I'll bet you anything you like that his version of these happenings will outlive mine, and that long after Jeremy and Grim and the Avenger and I are in our graves they will tell the story in El-Kalil of how Ali Baba made magic and destroyed a hundred thousand men.

THE END

www.ingramcontent.com/pod-product-compliance
Lightning Source LLC
Chambersburg PA
CBHW020134180626
46810CB00004B/1558